We Were Objects

Alen Gracen

Note From The Author

Dear Reader,

As an author I find that my work often consoles me when I'm feeling low. It gets me through the hard times to write and immerse myself into my worlds and characters. I hope you find that it might console you like it did me in whatever you might be going through, or that it might at least act as a lovely distraction. I hope you enjoy the story just as much as I enjoyed writing it. To all who end up reading, thank you so much for your time and support.

Alen Gracen

Content Warnings

Implications of animal abuse

Implications of self harm and implications of suicidal thoughts, both **_not_** experienced by the main characters.

To those who didn't let the actions

of others change their heart.

Chapter 1
Sean

The Object glowed in the darkness. He felt an overwhelming pull as it called to him. The bright light extended almost like arms wrapping around him, forcing him closer. The world around him seemed to blur and twist into darkness until the only thing he could see was the light. He extended his hand to it, feeling its energy at the tips of his fingers.

"Sean!" A familiar voice shattered through the darkness, but he couldn't name it. He was in far too deep to consider the consequences now. His fingers brushed the light and the object fully engulfed him. He felt the cold shock of the ground, and a warm familiar hand on his shoulder shaking him.

"Sean get up!" The voice came again, drawing him slowly away from the light and back into the darkness. The world around him came slowly back into his vision. The smell of the surrounding trees and the fog of the dark forest sending shivers across his body.

"I've got you." The voice grew more and more familiar by the second. He turned to face it.

"Tirin...?" The name came back to him suddenly. Tirin didn't respond, his dark eyes focused on dragging Sean to safety. Sean could feel his energy electric and shaky. He felt the churn of adrenaline the more he tried to read Tirin's emotions. He gently placed a hand on Tirin's shoulder, feeling his own calming energy course from his pendant into his chest, sending it through the tips of his fingers. Tirin's breathing slowed and he came to a stop in a large clearing, the darkness subsiding to the faint gleam of the fireflies.

"Thanks..." Tirin said after a deep breath. Suddenly he let go of Sean, thrusting him onto the ground, the grass meeting his face too soon for him to react. "What the hell was that?" He shouted at him.

"What...?" Sean tried his best to process what was happening around him. He searched his mind, the gentle hazy feeling lifting as the memories came flooding back to him.

"What were you thinking?! There is no way you actually touched it!" Tiring's voice seemed to shake the earth beneath them.

"The Object..." Sean said weakly.

"This is bad shit Sean!" Tirin's fists were white with rage. "You fucked up again!"

"Shut up already!" Sean snapped, feeling a burst of energy course through him. A burning sensation spread through his chest like wildfire.

"Not until you explain to me what the hell you were thinking." Tirin's intense gaze ripped through him.

"We don't have time for explanations. Where's Gem?" He shouted back.

"We're going to fucking make time Sean. You've just set the entire Sepratain force against us and you expect me not to ask questions?"

A small chunky black car drove into the clearing. The steady hum of the engine breaking up the conversation. The window rolled down and Gem's eyes shot a glare at them.

"You two can't be serious right now. Get in." She demanded. Both Sean and Tirin knew not to argue with Gem when she glared at them like that. They reluctantly climbed into the car, Sean in the backseat and Tirin on the passenger side. She rolled up the window and drove out of the clearing through the twist and turns of the forest like it was nothing. For a while they sat there in silence, the weight of the situation crashing down on them like a grand piano falling from the sky.

"That's the second time this week I've had to save your dumb asses, but I never once thought you could possibly fuck up this badly." Gem's voice broke through the silence.

"You can thank your brother for that." Tirin said bitterly. Sean felt the sting of salt in his tone.

"Alright I get it, I fucked up. Keep saying it, maybe it will make you feel better." He shot a glare at Tirin.

"I have every damn right to keep saying it. You mess up a lot, but touching the Sepratain Object? Are you out of your mind?" Tirin said.

"Don't act like you didn't stray from the plan first. I explained it to you about a hundred times and you still found a new way to veer off course. Who the hell chose you for fourth heir?" Sean hit him where he knew it would hurt.

"That's it! I'm done with this team. Once we get back to the warehouse, it's game over!" Tirin shouted.

"Don't you dare say that." Gem warned.

"You can't honestly tell me he's not being kicked off this time." Tirin spat.

Sean desperately wanted to say something, to shoot back a witty comment and argue his place in the team but he bit his tongue. He knew he had far extended his welcome now.

He'd messed up way worse than he ever thought possible. He'd put their lives in way more danger then they were already in. He felt as if had no right to even look at them anymore. Tirin grit his teeth, crossing his arms and turning to look out the window, satisfied with Sean's silence.

For the rest of the car ride the silence grew between them. Sean felt the harsh pain of guilt clench his heart to the point of breaking. He never once tried to speak, his anxiety getting the better of him. They reached the warehouse and the trio walked through the doors, splitting up. Tirin collapsed onto the couch with a long and exaggerated huff. Gem shuffled through the cabinets and drew out a bottle of Jack. Sean stared between them, looking back and forth before taking a deep breath and choosing to take a seat on the couch next to Tirin who refused to even acknowledge his presence.

After a long moment, Sean spoke. "Tirin I... Thank you..." His voice broke and his eyes pleaded for any ounce of understanding that usually never fell between them, but he was met with the same cold silence as Tirin stared at the wall in front of them, refusing to say a word. "I know I fucked up... and I don't even deserve the dam time of day from you but... I just need to know... why?"

Tirin sighed. "Don't flatter yourself. I was just looking out for the mission."

"But you didn't have to..." Sean didn't understand in the slightest Tirin's motivation for saving him. He could've just left him to be prosecuted.

What on this god forsaken planet had possessed him to go back for him?

His thoughts spiraled for a short moment before being interrupted again.

Tirin sank back into the couch giving another exaggerated sigh. "It doesn't matter now. We're all fucked."

"I'm sorry... I'm so sorry. If it's what you want I'll leave, I'll never say a word to you ever again." He slowly let down the walls he had been building up between them.

"Believe me I hate to admit it but, we're stuck together now, whether we like it or not," Tirin said bitterly, "so you might as well stop being so dramatic and get over it."

That last part almost sounded light hearted. Sean felt an overwhelming relief wash over him. He took a deep breath and let himself sink into the couch next to him. It wasn't any kind of forgiveness in the slightest, but it was a start, and he would gladly take whatever he could get. He gently fidgeted with his stringed bracelets. His eyes shot up and he almost jumped out of his seat as he realized there was a new one there that he had never seen. It was a thick leather strap, secured firmly in place. His initials engraved gold on the white of the surrounding color.

Tirin looked over and followed Sean's gaze. His eyes widened. "Holy shit..." He muttered.

Sean's voice came out breathless and his pulse quickened instantly. "The Object, it's bound to me."

***

For once, Gem's expression was unreadable. Sean had only ever seen that face one other time when they were teenagers. That was when the Hallow's family object was given to Sean instead of her. She had worked so incredibly hard, for nothing. She was far more equipped for the object then Sean could ever be, but their father couldn't fathom the idea of the object going to his daughter instead of his first born son, no matter how much of a failure Sean was. He'd hoped he'd never have to see that look again, but there it was.

"I know..." Sean tried to speak, to say anything to get her to react. "We don't have much time..."

"We're lucky they're not here already." Tirin added.

"What do we-"

"We have to unbind you." She interrupted Sean firmly.

"The Neutral object is nothing more than a legend." Tirin said.

"Got any other ideas? You'll go to the Neutralists Temple and plead for answers. I'll distract the VAA." The Vermillia Affairs Association or the VAA, was known for their dealings with Vermillia. They were an organization of regular people from the normal continent whose mission was to make sure, Sean's continent, Vermillia, didn't do anything too powerful. Normally they never intervened much, but ever since Antic was chosen as the heir to the Sepratain Object, they sent the trio to steal it. Even though all three of them were from the Necrotanian side of Vermillia, they each agreed for their own reasons, and Gem was the leader of the team. She had been a part of the VAA a lot longer than Tirin and Sean. She already covered for them in the past, but this time, covering could mean the end of her job and even worse, *imprisonment*.

"You can't. They'll lock you up instantly." Sean protested.

"It will give you some time to figure things out." She still managed to keep that same unreadable expression. Sean felt a churn in his stomach just looking at her.

"But-" Sean tried to argue but unlike Tirin, Gem never humored it. It was one of the reasons she made such a good leader.

"You're going and that's final." Sean looked into her eyes for a moment. The tension in the room almost materialized. He stepped closer, and the minute he did, he saw her falter. She instantly pulled him into a tight embrace, wrapping her arms protectively around him. When you see someone who always has it together hug you the way she hugged him in that moment, you break inside.

"Please, be safe. Don't do anything I wouldn't do." Sean could hear the firmness in her voice slipping away.

"We'll come back for you once this is over." He knew he might not be able to keep that promise, but he held onto her just a bit tighter for a long moment, her long white hair draping over his shoulder.

"You better." She pulled away slowly, her eyes shining with unshed tears. "Now go, before I get mad all over again."

For a brief moment they smiled at each other. Tirin didn't say a word, he just started walking out of the building. He never really took goodbyes well, or any emotional moment for that matter.

"That means he'll miss you." Sean chuckled. Gem didn't laugh, she just smiled as she watched Sean walk out of the warehouse. He could hear her breaking breath as he left, each distant sob etching cracks into his heart with the lingering thought that he might never see his sister again.

Chapter 2
Tirin

The damn idiot was walking way too slow. Tirin shoved his hands in his pockets as they walked through the rocky streets of Vermillia's center line. Sean followed not far behind, but Tirin didn't want to lose sight of him, especially now that he had the Sepratain object bound to him. He almost got taken by the Sepratain Forces back in the forest, and Tirin wasn't about to let anything like that happen to him again. Sean didn't seem to notice the way he kept looking back at him and huffing. His eyes focused on the buildings as they walked by, and it was obvious he was lost in his thoughts.

"Hey, idiot, pay attention." He demanded.

Sean seemed to snap out of it for a moment. He rolled his eyes. "What do you want?"

"You can't be lagging behind like that. We've got people on our tracks." Tirin slowed his walking pace until he was right next to Sean.

"Look, I'm not thrilled about this either—"

"Don't. I get it. A lot on your mind." He interrupted him. His eyes never left the scene around them, darting between the city's buildings, preparing for any signs of danger.

"Yeah..." Sean grew quiet. Tirin resisted a smirk watching the way he fidgeted with his stringed bracelets. He was way too easy to read.

"Relax, will you? We don't have room for you to be so distracted."

"Relax? At a time like this? You're insane." Sean said with a clear hint of envy at the way Tirin could so easily compose himself.

Tirin reluctantly let his smirk creep onto his face. "See that's the problem with you. You're always overthinking everything. That's what cost you the victory in the Necrotanian Trials." He knew bringing up the trials would hurt him, especially after getting him disqualified, and yet he couldn't help but rub it in.

Sean clenched his fists. "You played dirty."

Tirin's smirk widened seeing how clearly Sean still hadn't let it go. "Not my fault. Everyone has a weakness, you just have to press their buttons enough to get it to show." He shrugged like it was no big deal, even though he actually found the fight they had very difficult. Sean really gave him a challenge but there was no way in hell he'd ever admit that to him.

"Fuck off." Sean's tone grew more frustrated by the second.

"You're so easy to rile up, it's embarrassing."

Sean didn't respond. His eyes started to glow a dim white as he clenched his fists tighter by his sides. Tirin observed him closely, regarding how the object would react to his emotions. With all that power at his fingertips, Sean needed to learn to control it. Tirin knew first hand how dangerous an object could be without proper control. He struggled with his own object sometimes and that was only a fraction of the Necrotanian Object's power. He decided to push him further. "It's honestly pathetic that you think you could've ever been any kind of heir. You don't have an ounce of control in your body."

"I said fuck off." Sean's tone grew dangerous.

"Or what huh? You're going to fight me and cause a scene while we're on the run?"

Sean's eyes lit up with white light. Tirin didn't take his own eyes off him now. He dropped the act and spoke seriously. "What does it feel like? Pay attention to that feeling."

"What?" Sean snapped.

"Your eyes are lighting up. I know you feel the object's power." Sean's eyes seemed to dim for a moment as it dawned on him. He glanced at the leather strap on his wrist. It was firmly in place but Tirin could practically see the cogs ticking in Sean's mind. "Focus on it." He commanded.

Sean nodded and took slow deep breaths, closing his eyes for a brief moment. Though he was surprised Sean immediately listened to him, Tirin decided not to comment on it, smiling to himself instead.

"Don't summon anything here, but when the time comes, that's the feeling you need to rely on." The objects were used like a gateway to another world. Being bound to one meant you could summon creatures from that world, or certain abilities, like small blasts of energy. They manifested themselves into whatever form fit its user. Tirin's object had manifested itself as an earring he always wore on his right ear. He knew Sean would want to try it out, but there were laws around using objects. Summoning a creature in the centerline of the continent was bound to get them in trouble. For that reason, Tirin kept a careful eye on Sean as they walked.

The Neutralist temple wasn't far away now. Its gray stone walls could be seen in the distance, partially illuminated by the floating lanterns that always circled it. The light bounced off the stones as the lanterns danced around the structure. It was always said that the lanterns represented each member of the organization, but Tirin never really cared to pay attention to that anyways. As the fourth heir to the Necrotanian Object, which essentially meant fourth heir to the throne, his competitors always criticized him for his lack of knowledge regarding politics, telling him how important it was if he ever became more then just fourth in line, but he never saw himself ascending his position, no matter how badly he actually wanted it.

"Is that always how it feels?" Sean's voice interrupted his train of thought.

"What?"

"The object, I can feel it tingling and burning at my skin."

"You'll get used to it eventually, though the Necrotanian object tends to be more of a cold tingle. It's said that everyone feels it at varying intensities. Even then I've only got a small fraction of its power. I can't imagine how it feels for someone with the full object." Somehow there was a small hint of envy that he let slip in his voice.

"So it never stops?"

"Not once it's activated." Tirin raised an eyebrow at him. Sean should've known that. He'd been training for the object trials just as long as Tirin had. Though he knew it was an accident there was still a part of him that wondered if Sean had meant to fuck up the mission.

The Sepratain and the Necrotanian object were the two most powerful objects in the continent. Whoever was bound to them ruled the continent together in a dual monarchy system. The two sides of the continent were even named after the objects themselves. Seprati and Necrotan. Normally the heirs to the objects were decided by trials, that meant that even if Sean had stolen the object, he wasn't considered a rightful heir. Above all else, he'd be killed, not just for treason, but because there was no other way to unbind someone from an object. The Neutral object could theoretically help, but it was an object of legend. No one even really knew if it actually existed.

Still, there was a part of him that wondered if Sean had wanted to bind to the Sepratain object the whole time. "Can I ask you something?" Sean grew a concerned look and Tirin realized his words probably came out more sincere than usual. He rolled his eyes trying to play it off. "Is that a yes?"

"I guess."

"Tell me honestly. Did you mean what you did back there?"

"The apology?" Sean's expression softened. "Yeah…"

"Don't play dumb with me. I meant binding to the object." He scoffed, though part of him felt strange that Sean seemed so willing and open to speak about his apology back at the warehouse. The strange feeling only grew as Sean's face went pink with embarrassment.

"You honestly think I would've angered all of Seprati, and the VAA on purpose? You're even dumber than you look." His tone grew defensive.

"Well I don't know. You've always been salty about your loss at the trials. I wouldn't put it past you to desire something like that when you had a clear chance to bind to it. It's almost too perfect." Tirin started to remember the way he saw Sean reach for the object like he was in some sort of trance, even with Sepratian soldiers hot on their tail.

"I know what it looks like but I swear it isn't like that. I'm not that salty. I mean sure I've always wanted more power than my family heirloom gave me, but the Sepratian object was never in the cards for me before, especially with all my preparation for the complete opposite object matter. I mean the Sepratian and Necrotanian objects are nothing alike."

Sometimes families got hold of smaller objects that were passed down through generations. Those kinds of objects didn't act as links to another world, but simply as an amplifier to some smaller ability. Sean's family heirloom allowed him to read and influence other people's emotions. The Hallow's family object had been bound to him and manifested itself as a pendant Sean wore around his neck. Tirin often felt the ghost of Sean's hand on his shoulder and the calming energy it always pulsed through him, even when Sean wasn't around. It was a constant reminder that he was stuck working with him, and he hated it.

***

The steps leading up to the temple were polished and well kept. It made it difficult to climb them at a decent pace without slipping. Tirin had let Sean start the climb first so he could keep an eye on him. He seemed completely lost in his thoughts, focused on the new sensation of the object's power. Tirin knew that feeling too well by now.

Sean stumbled and almost fell backwards. Tirin put his hands up on instinct, as if preparing to catch him out of reflex. "I told you to focus but I didn't mean be carless." He said, his arms still extended as Sean steadied himself.

Sean shook his head rapidly and started back up the stairs. "Whatever."

Tirin had convinced himself that Sean's tendency to overthink things would one day get him killed, and that thought lingered for a moment as he put it into the context of the overwhelmingly delicate situation they were in. He decided right then and there that if they were going to be stuck together, he'd have to work extra hard to ensure their safety. He would do anything to break down the things in Sean's mind that held him back from the present moment and his own potential. For his own sake of course.

As they neared the top of the stairs, two women, dressed in all gray stood tall and intimidating at the entrance. One of them spoke, her tone low and suspicious. "State your business."

Tirin glanced at Sean. His own attempts at conversation usually always lead to hostility, so normally Sean was the one to speak to strangers. He spoke with a confidence that Tirin wished he had himself.

"We humbly request an audience with the Superior." Sean said in the most professional voice he could muster.

One of them waved a hand over the pair, assessing their magical allegiance, something all officials did as a custom to tell what side of the border you were from. "One Sepriti and one Necrotan." She said to the other. Sean and Tirin exchanged looks, realizing that Sean was now being read with Sepratian energy after binding to the object. Since they were both from Necrotan, neither of them were used to that at all.

The other taller woman stared at the pair for a moment before speaking. "A good balance." The two of them stepped aside and allowed the pair to pass through. Tirin caught Sean's small sigh of relief as they walked inside the two large double doors of the temple, but he held his breath. They weren't out of the woods yet.

They walked down a large entry hall with pillars on either side. The entire building was decorated with different shades of gray. There wasn't an ounce of color in sight other than the orange light of the floating lanterns, drifting around large painted portraits on the walls. He had a feeling he should've known some of the people in the portraits but he had very little knowledge of Neutralist history. The only thing he really knew was the current Superior's name, Ira Wander, and that she was a woman. He didn't know the first thing about her personality or even how she had been elected leader.

The Neutral object didn't work like the other ones. Both the Sepratain and the Necrotanian object were gateways to other dimensions. Other realities. Using the object's power meant calling on its energy or summoning creatures from another dimension, but the Neutral object didn't seem to work that way. At least that's what the Superior had said about it. That was part of why the movement had become more popular in recent days, the only other reason being how much people hated the next couple of heirs in line for the objects.

There was little known about where the actual object was or whether or not it's even real. The only person with the knowledge of where it might be was the Superior, and it stayed that way for generations. It was a long standing rumor that the Neutralist movement had just used it to base their religion off of and grow their power over others by enforcing that the head of the temple, the Superior, was the only person that knew where the Neutral object was.

Despite its size, the temple was surprisingly empty. The only sounds were the crackle of the lanterns and a quiet voice whispering across the great hall. The voice was coming from a woman dressed a bit more proper than the guards at the gate. Her dress was regal and glittered as he looked at it. Her eyes were glowing dimly and her dark hair was flowing long and loose along her shoulders. She didn't seem to notice the pair as they approached. She was standing tall with her hands extended towards a portrait in the center of the room.

Sean awkwardly cleared his throat, the sound echoing through the great hall. "Excuse me, can you point us to Ira Wander?"

"Who wishes to see her?" The woman's voice came out raspy, like she barely talked at all normally.

"Sean Hallow and Tirin... Uh..." Sean looked at Tirin, and he realized that Sean hadn't ever heard his last name before.

"Tirin Stirn." Tirin watched as Sean shifted his weight on his feet.

"Sean Hallow. Tirin Stirn." She repeated their names like she was analyzing them. She lifted her palm and scanned their allegiance. "So you want to see Ira?"

"Yes."

"Well, you're looking at her." The woman stood taller and fixed her posture as if she suddenly started to care more about her appearance.

"Right. Our apologies, we didn't recognize you." Sean said with a smile.

"That's quite alright." Her tone seemed a bit more casual now. "What brings you both here?"

"We need some very specific information, and it's very important that we get it." Tirin rolled his eyes as Sean spoke. He was beating around the bush.

"What kind of information?" She raised an eyebrow.

"You see, one of us has gotten into a complicated situation and-"

"We need to know where the Neutral object is." Tirin interrupted him, speaking in a blunt tone.

Ira's eyes widened. "What on earth could you need it for?"

Sean swallowed hard. "It's a bit complicated..."

"Sean accidentally bound to an object he didn't mean to bind to, and now we need to unbind it." Tirin finished for him again.

Ira's surprised look faded. It was clear she had heard that story many times before. "I would love to help you, but the location of the Neutral object is sacred, and I can't just give it out to strangers."

"I understand but please, this is very important..." Sean tried his best to reason with her, "If we don't unbind this object, a lot of very bad things could happen to us..."

"What kinds of bad things?" She was starting to sound suspicious of them. Tirin weighed the options in his mind. If they trusted her she could tell the Sepratain forces or the VAA where they were and where they had gone. She could even lie to them about where the Neutral object was. He thought harder for a moment. She was a Neutralist, and it was written in their core values not to get involved. Maybe she wouldn't betray them but that didn't mean she would help them either.

"That's equally as complicated…" Sean struggled to explain,

Tirin took a deep breath, briefly feeling the ghost of Sean's hand on his shoulder before speaking. "Ira, I know this is going to sound absolutely insane but Sean is bound to the Sepratian Object. As in *the* Sepratian object. If we don't unbind him soon, a lot of things are going to start falling apart."

Ira didn't look convinced at all. "*You* are bound to the Sepratian object? How is that possible?"

"We really don't have time to explain." Tirin said impatiently.

Sean lifted up his wrist, showing the white leather strap. Ira held a hand over it to sense its power. Tirin watched as her eyes stayed wide, but her tone was the same. "So, Sean Hallow, you challenged Antic Winter for heir?"

When it came to Antic, the next heir to the Sepratian object, people either really hated him or really loved him, and there was no in between. The previous rulers had emphasized unity between the two sides of the continent, especially after the border between them had been broken down a few generations ago, but Antic didn't agree on that matter. During his coronation speech he'd emphasized wanting to reinforce the border along with putting more restrictions on the VAA. He also believed the normal continent wasn't meant to have much say in the business of Vermillia, and the VAA, the association that dealt with relations between the continents, would get caught in the crossfire. Tirin didn't know Antic personally, but something about the way he smiled with his lips thinned in photos just rubbed him the wrong way. He saw him the night of the accident after Sean touched the object, and he knew he must've been furious, but it didn't show on his face.

Tirin oddly respected a guy who didn't show signs of weakness, but all that respect faded away instantly when he'd made his position on the new border laws adamant. He wasn't just the heir to the Sepratain object. He was determined to bring a new wave to the continent, a movement that would force the two sides of the continent apart. He didn't admit outright that he thought Sepratian people were far better than Necrotanian people, but it wasn't hard to tell how he felt.

"Not exactly..." Sean said weakly. Tirin noticed the way he shifted uncomfortably at the mention of Antic. He always seemed to tense up when his name was around. Despite his better judgment, Tirin had always assumed it was just because he didn't agree with his new policies.

"Look, even if you are now the heir, that doesn't change much for us as Neutralists. We do not act unless things are out of balance." She insisted.

"And what situation would you consider out of balance?" Tirin shot her a glare.

"The only reason I'd ever intervene is if someone with Necrotanian allegiance was bound to it."

Tirin huffed out a laugh and smirked. "Is that so?"

Sean elbowed him in the gut. "I hate to break it to you, but I am not from Seprati... not even close."

She stared at both of them and Tirin bit his tongue, holding himself back from punching Sean in the face after he'd elbowed him.

"That's ridiculous." She held her hand up trying to sense his allegiance again. Sean uncovered his family pendant from around his neck.

"See? The Hallow family." He gestured for her to sense it and she seemed visibly uncomfortable for a moment. Clearly she was originally from Seprati. Tirin had always felt that they were the more judgey and stuck up part of the continent and whether that was fully true or not didn't matter to him.

"That's unacceptable. You've tainted the balance." She said urgently.

"Now you understand. We need the Neutral object to fix this mess."

She let out a frustrated sigh and pinched the bridge of her nose. "I'll tell you what I know, but you aren't going to like it."

Sean perked up and she gestured for the pair to follow her down the hall. Tirin followed a small bit behind them silently. He listened in, but he was more focused on looking out for any signs of someone after them. He knew that Antic and the Sepratian forces wouldn't rest until they were caught. He could feel a small bit of anger rising inside as he thought about the situation they were in again. *Dam it Sean*. The thought pierced his mind as easily as the familiar fire of rage burned in his chest. He recognized when his emotions were threatening to boil. He took a deep breath, briefly trying to feel the ghost of Sean's hand on his shoulder. It worked. *It always worked.* That thought only made his anger flare back up just as quickly as it dissipated.

"Is that correct? Or am I missing something?" Sean looked back and gestured at Tirin to interject into the conversation that he absolutely hadn't been following. Sean's eyes read him. Tirin hated that feeling. The feeling when Sean read his emotions, his weaknesses, as easy as a kindergarten level picture book.

Sean tensed his shoulders and effortlessly continued the conversation. "Oh right I did forget that you dragged me out by the shirt." He chuckled lightly and Tirin realized they were talking about how Sean had bound to the object. He grew more frustrated. That wasn't important. Sean had no reason to share the details with Ira. He felt his hands tingle with the cold prick of his object's power.

"I see. That sounds very illegal." Ira said flatly.

"That isn't anyone's concern." Tirin said.

"Well it is now. You need my help, and you've thrown off the balance. I will give you the location, but there is more you will need to know about the Neutral Object itself." Her voice was almost mechanical at this point. Suddenly, Tirin seemed to appreciate the way she showed no emotion, no weakness. He respected people like that. Maybe he should've been a Neutralist. He shrugged that thought aside, remembering his family history and his tendency to overexert his powers. Neither of those were good traits for a Neutralist to have.

Ira walked them over to a room at the end of the great hall. It had a small door with a coded padlock on it. She typed in some numbers and the door unlocked with a buzzing sound. Sean backed up until he was standing next to Tirin. He leaned over his shoulder and whispered to him.

"Getting riled up won't help us here." He offered his hand to use his family object on him.

Tirin bit back a scowl. "I can handle myself."

Sean shot him a glare. He could tell there was more he wanted to say. Probably something like a denial and a sharp insult, but Ira waved them in through the door behind her and Sean obliged. Tirin again followed behind, glancing around them cautiously.

The room was set up like a mini library. Shelves organized in a sort of archive system were along the walls. Books, scrolls, documents, files, and any other kind of method one could use to hold information all sprawled around the room. Ira walked over to a lock box, neatly placed on a desk in the corner of the room, and drew out a small key from underneath her dress. Tirin tried not to focus on the fact that she had kept the key against her chest underneath the glittery fabric.

A moment later she opened the box and drew out a scroll. It looked old and torn, tinted by pure age. She spoke lightly. "This is the only thing the last ten generations of Superiors have had in regards to the whereabouts of the Neutral object."

She opened the scroll and placed it on the desk in front of them. There was a written location of coordinates and a single line of warning written in dark red. *Protected heavily.*

"That's it?" Sean said.

"It is a location. That's all it needs to be." She rolled up the scroll delicately and drew out a clean piece of paper, copying the coordinates and warning neatly. She then folded the paper and handed it to Sean.

"Thank you so much for your time." Sean said.

"A pleasure." She said flatly, then gestured for the pair to leave.

Tirin's eyes never left their surroundings as they left the temple. He knew Sean could see the caution practically radiating off him and it strongly annoyed him. His watchful eyes never stopped pouring into his weaknesses as if he wasn't allowed a sense of privacy.

As they walked back down the slippery steps Tirin spoke, "Stop staring at me and just say it already."

"Say what? You aren't going to let me help you anyways." Sean rolled his eyes and focused on his steps.

"Then look at something else." He demanded.

"Like what? The sky? Or how about the fact that two entire civil forces are after us? Great idea." The sarcasm spilled out of him like acid.

"Anything other than me." He said frustrated. Truthfully he would rather Sean focus on him then worry and let his new power get out of control but there was no way he'd admit that. Sean already knew his weaknesses, he didn't need anything else.

"I'm just trying to help you."

"I don't need your help."

"Look, it's not like it's charity. You saved my ass back in Seprati, just let me return the favor." That was the only thing Sean was actually good for. He was good at convincing people and getting his way.

Tirin sighed. "If I let you, will you stop reading my emotions like that? It's an invasion of my privacy."

"Deal." Sean lifted his hand slowly to his shoulder, not hesitating for a second. In one small breath, he drew the power from his pendant into his hand. Tirin felt a wave of calm pass through his shoulder. A small tingling burst spread through his body making him sigh in relief. After a few deep breaths Sean withdrew his hand.

"There, was that so hard?"

"Yes." Tirin had intended the comment to come out bitterly, but the effect of the object had him speaking level headedly. He felt a small fog pass in his mind. He couldn't even remember what he was thinking before.

They continued walking back through Vermillia's center line, the city around them decently alive at that time of night. Tirin continued to keep a relaxed eye on Sean.

After a good ten minutes a man dressed in travel clothing gripped Tirin's arm harshly.

"Tirin Stirn, Sean Hallow, you're under arrest by the authority of the VAA." He announced suddenly.

"You've got to be kidding me." Tirin rolled his eyes. Thinking one could restrain the fourth heir to the Necrotanian object by simply gripping his arm was entirely stupid.

"Any attempt made to resist will be—" Tirin cut him off, grabbing his arm and practically throwing him forward. In an instant, a bunch of the surrounding civilians, clearly disguised VAA agents, turned on them, stun weapons drawn.

"You will come peacefully." One of them said.

"And that's our cue." Sean announced, smirking.

Tirin nodded and almost instantly felt his object power course through him from his earring into his eyes. He projected it through his hands in a burst of dark matter. A large dark circle appeared above them, black ooze practically dripping out of it. The people around them focused their immediate attention on the circle as a large skeletal creature came crawling out of it. A screech echoed from its mouth through the city center. Shots instantly fired at the creature from all directions. Tirin grabbed Sean's wrist, practically dragging him along as he pushed people out of the way. The remaining civilian's around them started scrambling in panic.

"I thought you were better than that." Sean muttered under his breath.

"You're already bound to the object, there isn't really any worse crime than that."

"Yeah, that absolutely excuses releasing a large Necrotanian creature in the center of the city." He knew the action was completely illegal and dangerous, but he couldn't bring himself to care at that moment. "Got any better ideas?" His grip on Sean's wrist tightened. "It's your fault we're in this mess in the first place."

Sean didn't even have time to respond as one of the civilian dressed agents nearly shot the pair with a stun gun. He ducked under it, allowing the blast to hit another agent.

The agent shook for a moment then fell to the ground feeling a shockwave course through them. With ease, Tirin commanded the creature to his side. The boney creature kicked and thrusted people across the street with its arms. With each hard hit, a few of its bones flew off, leaving the shell of a figure protecting them. The pair made a break for it, running left from the center line into Seprati.

After taking a few turns and running as far as they could get, Tirin allowed the creature to retreat back to its world, but he didn't stop walking, still holding tightly onto Sean's wrist.

"You don't have to hold on so tight." He complained.

Tirin ignored him and kept speed walking, dragging him along. "We're lucky the VAA has no idea what they are dealing with. That won't be the last time either. We need to keep moving."

"Moving to where exactly? We haven't even plugged in the coordinates yet." Sean protested, yanking his hand back and forcing Tirin to stop walking for a moment.

"Anywhere but here. We can worry about coordinates when we are far enough away." He said quickly.

"What if we are running in the wrong direction? Won't that set us back?" Sean stubbornly stood still glancing at a nearby shop. "And don't you think we should have some sort of disguise or something?"

Tirin grunted, annoyed with Sean's inability to keep moving without overthinking everything. At some point he had to reluctantly consider his argument. They also needed supplies, it's not like they could just run around the continent with nothing but the clothes on their backs.

"One store, then we leave." He said begrudgingly. Just because Sean was right, didn't mean he had to give in without his own terms.

"That one." Sean pointed to a building well known in the area. A standard mart with the materials they would likely need.

If it didn't hit him yet, Tirin was finally coming to realize just how long he was about to be stuck with the most annoying person in the world. Just his luck.

Chapter 3
Sean

Sean considered it a good thing he had experience with survival and tracking, but damn did he hate the way Tirin seemed to be good at everything. The light from the GPS device blinked red indicating 2 days travel on foot. It wouldn't be all that bad despite the ever changing weather patterns of the Sepratain forest, except that the pair couldn't agree on a single thing, not even the walking pace.

"If we go too fast, we'll be tired before dusk." Sean muttered. He decided to play a mental game with himself, guessing the number of times Tirin would complain about something he was doing wrong. So far in the span of one hour, he had counted 13 times. His overall guess for the night, 60, which he thought completely reasonable.

"How many times do I have to remind you we have people after us?" And there he went again, acting like Sean didn't realize the harsh situation they were in.

"I'm not stupid. I know that," He snapped, "I'm just saying we don't want to get tired out too quickly."

Tirin huffed and stared at the small overgrown path ahead. To Sean's surprise he left it at that. It didn't stop him from walking ahead of him though, which in turn meant that Sean had the privilege of staring at the back of his head the rest of the way. He could've easily gotten lost in his thoughts again, but he thought it was a good idea to avoid that for now.

Tirin's dark curls fell on top of his head, shaved into a fade along the sides. His broad shoulders pierced the air around him. The intense gaze of his dark eyes stared straight ahead, never leaving the surrounding area. That was the way he always looked when he was uneasy. By now Sean knew all of his emotional mannerisms, from the darting of his eyes to the slight lift of his chin, but that didn't make it any easier to get close to him. Tirin's walls were built higher than any Sean had ever seen. His emotional state was constantly clouded when Sean tried to read him. His emotional aura swirled and bloomed around like smoke from a raging fire.

Reading people's emotions was like second nature at that point. Sean did it without thinking, even though it was sort of an invasion of privacy. He often felt bad for doing it, especially when Tirin called him out for it, but he couldn't help it. It was in his nature, and out of everyone, Tirin was the most interesting person to read. No matter how hard he tried, he could never fully understand what Tirin was feeling unless it was anger. His energy was unclear and foggy. Even right then and there Sean could only make an educated guess based on his body language alone.

There were only three emotions Tirin showed at a decently readable level. The first and easiest to read was anger, the second was artificial calm Sean created for him, and the third was a strange sense of paranoia he almost always carried with him. It was like he thought the world was out to get him, even if he never expressed it out loud. For a guy who seemed so in control of himself, Sean found it odd that Tirin's paranoia got through his walls every single time they were alone. It seemed hypocritical how much Tirin constantly told him to relax.

"You know, maybe you should take your own advice sometime." Sean spoke up.

"What?"

"You need to relax."

Tirin rolled his eyes. "What about me doesn't look relaxed right now?"

"I'm not blind. You're acting like we'er about to get jumped." Sean didn't want to explain how he was reading him, but he wouldn't be able to hide it for long.

"If you're trying to read me, cut it out" Sean almost instantly read the frustration radiating off him. It was like the smoke came up through the foggy aura around him. The kind of smoke that contaminated the air.

"Would you rather me focus on all the forces after us?"

Tirin let out a harsh breath somewhere between a huff and a laugh. "Honestly? Yes."

"You're impossible to please." Sean threw his hands in the air, defeated.

"As if you care about pleasing me."

He found himself about to fall for that trap. Of course he cared about Tirin's well being. He might be an asshole but it's not like Sean wanted him to die. Still he recognized the reaction he almost acted on.

"Oh, that's right, I only exist to annoy you." He resorted to sarcasm instead.

"Keep talking and you'll only prove that to be true." Tirin exhaled.

"You know, time might move faster if we talk." Sean said, rolling his eyes.

"Can't we just walk in silence? It's peaceful."

"Silence isn't peaceful."

"It is if you tell your brain to shut up." Tirin huffed out a laugh.

"You act like that's an easy thing to do." Sean shot him a glare.

"It is."

"If it's so easy then why are you always so paranoid?" The question seemed to catch Tirin off guard.

"Paranoid?"

"Don't play dumb with me. It's obvious."

"I knew it," Tirin grit his teeth, "You are reading me aren't you." Sean could see the way the smoke clouded more of his emotional energy. Whatever was in the foggy aura was now being overrun and hidden by Tirin's frustration.

"We've talked about this... I can't help it."

"Control yourself." Tirin demanded.

"I am in control." Sean cursed himself. Of course he was in control, he just wanted to read him so painfully bad. He never got that way with other people, but something about Tirin made him focus on his abilities more.

"Then stop being an asshole and pay attention to your own damn emotions." He said flatly.

"What are you so afraid of?" Unless Tirin expressed it himself, any hope of figuring out his paranoia was gone now.

"Like I said, silence would be nice right about now."

"Fine." Sean sighed. He was slowly starting to accept that he wouldn't get anything out of him. Apparently they were destined to keep the same animosity between them forever.

***

The pair had been walking the entire day, not stopping for a single break. Sean's feet were aching, but that wasn't an excuse enough for Tirin to let him rest. Finally they found a place to set up camp in a small clearing. Sean started to set up the one tent they had, but Tirin continued to criticize his every action until he gave up and let him do it himself. He sat on the ground, watching Tirin with an annoyed expression. The worst part was Tirin knew what he was doing. He made putting together a tent look effortless.

"You sleep on one side, I'll sleep on the other." Tirin said, stepping back for a moment to pull out his sleeping bag.

Sean chuckled at the possibility of any other sleeping arrangement. Of course he would be as far to the opposite side of the tent as physically possible. "You act like I'm going to try and cuddle you or something."

Tirin shot him a glare. "Don't even think about it."

"Trust me, I won't." Sean rolled his eyes and got out his own sleeping bag.

"I'll take the first watch." Tirin said flatly.

"Right." That was the last thing he said. The silence grew until Sean practically forced himself to close his eyes and drift off to sleep. Except sleep, the thing everyone needs as part of human existence, didn't come. At least not nearly enough of it. He probably managed around 2 hours before Tirin woke him for the next watch.

He sat on the ground outside of the tent, irritated with himself. The surrounding wilderness was alive with sounds of bugs, small creatures and a light breeze. The misty smell served as an odd means of comfort. Familiar in a way. He'd been around that smell most times his family went camping when he was a boy. Gem would always claim she could do things better than him, but his parents wouldn't let her near a fire pit.

He added a few sticks to the small dim light of the fire, keeping it steady. As much as he didn't like the heat of it, it sort of kept him awake to know something was burning right next to him. For the past 20 minutes he had been hearing light rustles of grass and breaking of a few twigs on the ground. He had seen a few small rabbits hopping through so when the current sounds hit his ears, he paid no mind to them. Still he looked in that direction, wanting to spot the cute animals. That's when a voice startled him.

"Well, look who we have here." The voice was deep, familiar but with some kind of edge he didn't recognize.

"Who's there?" He said, almost instantly clutching his pendant.

"You know who I am Sean. You knew I was coming." He heard a cracking sound straight in front of him. A relatively tall, dark shadow of a man shifted, making his position known.

"What do you want?" Sean still couldn't place who it was, but he decided that part didn't matter.

"You know the answer to that. I want what you took from me." That's when it clicked. *Antic.* "Did you tell your friend about us?" Sean froze. Of course he'd left that part out. Tirin would absolutely murder him if he found out how close he used to be with Antic. "I'm going to take that as a no. You never had the decency to be honest with people."

"I was honest with you. I always have been." Sean slowly began to stand.

"Don't even think about it. I've been done with your lies for quite some time now." Antic came out from the darkness, standing tall. He clutched his own necklace, primed and ready for attack if needed. The black of his hanging chains standing out against his white outfit. Sean swallowed hard before continuing to his feet.

Antic took a step forward, his tone warning. "You know I'm not dumb enough to come out here alone."

"So what are you going to do? Kill me?" Sean knew the answer to that. The object was bound to him. There was literally no other way to solve things.

"Don't be an idiot. If I wanted you dead I would've killed you already. I'm the heir to the Sepratain object, remember?" He made a breathy sound, somewhere between a laugh and a harsh exhale.

"So what then?"

"So you're coming with me Sean," he smirked, "And you're going to do exactly as I say."

"I'm not sure why you think he's going anywhere with you." Tirin's voice broke the tense air between them. He came out of the tent and stood by Sean's side.

"I'm not sure who Sean associates himself with now, but you don't have to have any part in this. Leave him to me and you can go without consequence."

Tirin looked between the pair. Sean cursed under his breath. Of course Tirin would take the offer. All Sean had ever done was annoy him and create problems for him.

The tension in the air materialized for a long moment. Sean watched as Tirin glared at him.

"Wait a minute. This is personal isn't it?" There it was again. The dark cloud that followed Tirin wherever he went. The only emotion that could be read clear as day.

"Oh, that's right. You're little fuck up here hasn't been honest with you." Antic mocked him, as if that was the first time that night he'd mentioned it.

"I promise this isn't what it looks like..." Sean tried to explain himself, but how could he?

"It's exactly what it looks like and you know it Sean." Antic said flatly.

"Sean?" Tirin read his eyes. He hated that. Is that what it felt like to be read? No wonder Tirin hated it when he read him. He couldn't say a word to him. The familiar stab of guilt pierced his stomach.

"My offer still stands." Antic reminded him.

Tirin looked between the pair one last time. For a moment Sean thought he might actually surprise him. That hope hadn't been rewarded back at the warehouse, but *maybe this time* he told himself.

Tirin's expression fell flat. "A pleasure, Antic." He turned, walking back into the tent. Sean crunched inward. He expected that, sure, but he hadn't expected it to hurt. Not like his insides were being ripped apart.

"Likewise." Antic nodded, his eyes starting to glow as he clutched his necklace tighter. He turned his attention back to Sean. "Like I said, you never had a good choice in friends." Sean clenched his fists, his own eyes starting to glow. He'd felt the burning sensation before. He focused on it.

"Now don't go trying something stupid. Come with me willingly and this won't have to get messy." As he spoke, a number of Sepratain force soldiers came out from the surrounding darkness, circling the space around them. He weighed the options in his head. It was either, be taken back to Seprati and most likely be tortured by his ex best friend and killed, or fight back with an object's power he didn't know how to control and risk being killed sooner.

He paused his thoughts for a moment, a new one entering. *Why did he need Sean alive? Surely it wasn't just to torture him.* He knew Antic better than that. There had to be a reason. Whatever he wanted, maybe he could leverage it somehow. Now he just needed a way to bring it out of him.

"Oh, I get it. You can't kill me." Sean smiled, playing up his confidence.

Antic hummed. "What makes you say that?"

"You still care about me. Deep down."

"Whatever part of me that cared about you was shattered that day. I could kill you right now." He frowned.

"Then why don't you? You want me to suffer or something so you can feel better?" Now he was taunting him. He felt nerves churn in his stomach at the level of dangerous insanity he was playing with. "You want to teach me a lesson I'll never act on?"

Sean saw him falter. He made that same face he always made when he was contemplating. "Whatever information I need out of you isn't worth your little games. Maybe

I should just kill you where you stand." The glow in his eyes intensified.

"Then do it. At least then you'll be done with me right?" Sean let go of his pendant and spread out his arms. He exposed his chest as a perfect target. If that was where it had to end, he would accept it. He deserved it after everything he'd done to worsen the lives of the people he cared about.

"Any last words?" Antic extended an open palm to him. The glow in his eyes traveled through his arm slowly until it was at the tips of his fingers.

"I've always cared about you, even if it wasn't in the way you wanted it." Sean made one last attempt to be honest with him, even if he wouldn't change. Even if he died right then and there, at least he would've gotten his closure of expressing what he wanted to say to him all this time.

"Liar." Antic shot a large burst of energy from the palm of his hands. The white light blinded the entire space around them, lighting up the dark of the night. He felt the scorching pain of the blast hit him. *Is this what it feels like to be free of the guilt that drowns me?*

Chapter 4
Tirin

Of course he didn't take the deal. Antic wouldn't leave him alone and he knew that. Taking his offer only meant he'd deal with him later after he had the object back from Sean. *After Sean died.* No matter how much he hated him, that just didn't sit right. And what was all that about caring for him? The dam screw up just forgot to mention that Antic had a personal vendetta against him? *Great.* If he had to stick with him, he wasn't about to admit it, much less announce it to the opposing party. What kind of idiot did Sean think he was? Still he couldn't bite back the way the look in Sean's eyes destroyed him. The guilt on his face, the begging in his voice. He hated it, but deep down he knew that was the real reason he was there in the VAA's medical wing, sitting by his side.

The medic explained to him and Gem about a hundred times that he was fine. The blast had knocked him out and apparently wasn't intended to be lethal. The worst that he'd walk away with was a few surface level burns. That didn't stop Gem from pacing back and forth in the room.

Tirin sighed. He had forced himself not to ask any questions, but now he couldn't handle it. "You knew, didn't you."

Gem looked at him sideways, pausing her pace. "Knew what?"

"You knew he had a history with Antic and you just decided to leave that part out?"

She shrank into herself, visibly uncomfortable. "It wasn't relevant."

He raked a hand through his hair. "How is that not relevant?"

"It wasn't, until the plan went sideways."

He relaxed his posture, deciding to let it go. He had no business in Sean's history at the moment, and he knew he could get him to spill the second he woke up. That was the second time he saved his life after all. He figured he was owed some kind of explanation at least. Sean, passed out on the hospital bed, seemed to be sleeping peacefully. Every now and then he would shift or make some small sound that Tirin could barely catch. He convinced himself that being by his side for hours had more to do with his lack of something to do than anything else. He found himself staring at that peaceful expression that struck him differently. It was similar to the one he wore when he was using his abilities to calm him. He was so caught up in his thoughts he almost didn't notice when Sean's eyes squinted open.

"Well look who's finally awake." He made his awakened state known for Gem who came over by his side in an instant.

"Don't scare me like that idiot." She said, Sean didn't seem to be fully processing what was going on. He rubbed his eyes gently. "I didn't think he'd actually..." His voice came out a bit shaky.

"That was stupid." Tirin remarked. He looked up at him. He held his gaze for a moment. "Yeah, you've got some explaining to do."

"Did you— wait. Where are we?" Sean's eyes darted around the room as he became more aware of the situation.

"VAA Headquarters. At least, the headquarters in Vermillia." Gem said as she began checking Sean's eyes and face, examining him as if she was the medic.

"How did we get here?"

"That's complicated but the gist of it is, I saved your life. Again." Tirin figured he could at least brag about it once.

"Antic... actually tried to kill me..." Sean clearly hadn't realized Antic wasn't going to spare his life, but to Tirin that was stupid. Antic wanted the object and the only way to get it was to kill Sean. Of course he was going to try and kill him. He thought it was obvious for a minute before remembering that they supposedly had a history. That's what happened when people got emotionally involved. He wasn't stupid enough for that. He wanted to make a remark about it, but he figured now wasn't the time. They had more important things to deal with.

"The medic said the blast wasn't intended to be lethal." Gem tried her best to reassure him. Sean's face visibly relaxed. It was like the thought of Antic wanting to kill him haunted him somehow. Tirin's curiosity for their history grew by the second.

He raised an eyebrow. "To me that doesn't make any sense."

"I think you mean, thank goodness he didn't kill you." Sean rolled his eyes.

"Back to the attitude so soon? I thought I'd have more time before you regained your sense of annoyance."

Sean crossed his arms. "Well you thought wrong."

Tirin decided he would never get over the way he spoke like a child at times. "So he didn't kill you. That doesn't mean he'll stop chasing us."

Gem visibly relaxed a bit seeing Sean acting normal again. "Did you figure out where the Neutral object is?"

"Sort of. We met up with the superior Ira wander and—"

"We have a set of coordinates we were following and a warning." Tirin cut him off, deciding Gem didn't need the entire story. Sean shot him a glare.

Gem rolled her eyes before continuing the conversation. "A warning?"

"You thought recovering an object of legend would be easy? Of course it's protected somehow." He showed her the copied text.

"I see."

"Once we're done here we can get back on track." Sean shifted impatiently.

"Nope. The VAA isn't just going to let you waltz out of here."

Sean shrank into himself. "Are we going to jail or something?"

"Not exactly. They are mad about the mission, but at the same time they'd rather you have the object than Antic."

"Good so we can just go."

"Of course not. After almost getting captured, they think it's too risky to let you go."

"So I'm just going to keep the object?"

Tirin rolled his eyes. "No idiot. Obviously they are going to send us or other agents to find the Neutral object while you stay here under their protection."

Sean looked at Gem as if waiting for her to tell Tirin he was wrong, but all she did was nod along. Sean grew quiet. It was the kind of quiet Tirin had seen in him before. One that meant he would be tangled in his own thoughts for the next couple of hours.

"It's for the best." Gem said. She put a hand on his shoulder. "It's not that bad here. You can keep yourself busy."

"Are you going to go?" Sean looked up at her, like an absolute child asking their sibling not to leave them alone.

"Yes. They trust me. You two, not so much after that mission."

Sean grew an annoyed expression. "So not only will I be stuck here, but I'll be stuck here with him?"

Despite the situation, Tirin couldn't help but smirk at the idea of getting to pester the annoying guy as pay back for the mission. "Oh we're going to have a blast." His voice oozed with sarcasm.

Gem looked between them and shook her head. "Just try not to kill each other, OK?"

A tall man dressed in the VAA uniform peaked his head through the door. "Hallow, you ready?"

Gem stood from her spot next to the hospital bead. "I'll see you soon." She smiled before walking out of the room. For a long moment there was just silence. Sean's same thoughtful expression was painted on his face. Tirin stayed silent. He observed him. It was easy to read him as usual. His eyebrows pinched, his expression somber. Even the way his breathing slowed.

"I guess I owe you a thanks. Again." Sean broke the looming silence.

"You don't owe me anything. I was just doing my job."

"I know that's not it. Don't lie to me. You could've left me. Antic would've left you alone and you could have been rid of me." Sean looked him in the eyes, that sharp soul boring gaze. "I thought you hated me."

"I do hate you." He made sure to say it flatly. "You mess up everything, you're weak with your abilities, and to top everything off, you were hiding your history with Antic from me."

"If that's true then why?"

Tirin paused. *Why did he save him?* Maybe it was that look in his eyes, that tremble in his voice. Maybe it was the way he saw part of his younger self in him. He sighed. "You know Antic wouldn't have actually left me alone. My image is bound to you now, whether I'm the fourth heir to the Necrotanian object or not."

"But you would've dealt with Antic without me."

"Not after he killed you for the object. That would make him stronger and-" He paused, annoyed with himself.

"And?"

"And letting him kill you just doesn't seem right."

Sean looked at him, searching his gaze for something. Tirin shifted, slightly uncomfortable, but decided to hold his gaze.

"You don't want me dead?"

"Look I might be an ass but I'm not heartless." He rolled his eyes. *Honestly, is that what Sean thought of him?* What an idiot.

"You are absolutely an ass." There was the usual insult but there was something different attached to it. Something Tirin wasn't used to. Then as if it couldn't get any more confusing, Sean smiled. Sean *never* smiled at him like that. "It's nice to know you're not a monster.

"Don't mistake my words for friendship moron." He crossed his arms.

"I wouldn't dare." Sean continued to smile. It rubbed Tirin the wrong way. He wanted him to stop. He wanted to wipe that stupid grin off his face.

"We're both stuck with the VAA and you're smiling like an idiot."

"Oh I'm sorry, guess I'll go back to moping around." Sean laughed. A small innocent laugh. Something light-hearted to it.

"I preferred that. At least then you were quiet." Tirin raised an eyebrow. "And you better not be reading me. It's bad enough that you lied to me. I don't need you invading my personal emotions too."

Sean's expression changed. "Ok. I know I hid it from you. Can you really blame me? If you knew it was personal there was no way you would've helped us with the mission, and I didn't think I would actually end up facing him like that... " Sean paused. "I didn't think he would actually hurt me."

"How could you have gotten that part so wrong? I saw that look in his eyes. That guy wants you to suffer. I've only ever seen that kind of look once."

"He's never been like that. He'd never hurt me. And technically he didn't, he just knocked me out."

It was easy to see past Sean's naivety. There's a kind of hope that comes from broken things. A kind of hope that makes you believe you can fix them. It only comes easy to those who know to ignore that instinct based on personal experience. It always hurts the worst the first time. Tirin was no stranger to that hope. He'd let it die a long time ago.

"Sean. He wanted to hurt you. He didn't right then and there, but he was going to. I don't know what happened between you, but that's not how someone who doesn't want to hurt people looks. Regardless if he just knocked you out, what was he going to do then? Makeup with you? He said he wanted to hurt you, plain as day."

Sean's gaze fell to the bed. "I refuse to believe that."

"I know it hurts, but if you ever listen to anything I say, let it be this. He wants you dead."

"First you say you don't want me dead, and now you're giving me some odd kind of advice? Who are you and what have you done with the asshole that got me disqualified at the trials?"

Tirin rolled his eyes again. He recognized the change of subject, but decided not to push it. Those kinds of things took time to unravel. "Don't get used to it."

"I wouldn't dream of it."

"And I didn't get you disqualified. You got yourself disqualified, I just provoked you."

Sean crossed his arms. "Still your fault."

"Keep telling yourself that."

***

The rest of the day went by with an excruciating slowness. Most of it consisted of training the use of the objects and bugging the shit out of Sean. As awful as Sean was at using the newly acquired power, Tirin managed to teach him how to channel a small burst of energy through his palms. It helped that he had watched Antic do it with the same type of power. By night fall, they had both been given specific rooms to sleep in on the east side of the VAA headquarters. They weren't really put under intense watch but it was made clear that they weren't allowed to leave the facility freely.

After spending the entire day with the annoying prick, Tirin was thankful he finally got some time to himself. He cleaned himself up, took a nice hot shower, and settled into his bed to relax. He took in a few deep breaths, bringing his thoughts to a slow pace. He almost relaxed fully if it hadn't been for the steady knocking that shook him out of his relaxation. He grunted, forcing himself off the bed. He opened the door to Sean, staring at him. Of course it was Sean.

"What do you want?" Sean's eyes were fixed on Tirin's chest. Tirin looked down at him before realizing he had forgotten he didn't have a shirt on. "What? Never seen a chest before?"

Sean shook himself out of it quickly. "No! I just wanted to talk about our escape."

"Our what?"

Sean pushed him back into the room and shut the door behind him. The sudden feel of Sean's hands on his bare chest causing him to grab his arms on impulse.

"Relax. Don't tell me you thought we were actually going to stay here with the VAA."

Tirin looked down at Sean's hands still on his chest. "Does it look like I was prepared to leave?"

"Seriously? No way I'm letting Gem have all the fun while I sit around bored."

Tirin exhaled sharply. "And you just expect me to go with you? What about the guards at the door? What about the cameras? How do you think the VAA is going to react when we show up at the site of the Neutral object? Do you even have any plans at all?"

He lifted his hands and poked a finger to the center of his chest. "Of course I have a plan. Not that you know how to stick to things like that."

"Ok smart ass, what's your plan?"

Sean looked him up and down. "First put some clothes on and meet me in my room."

"Fine, but if I get there and you don't actually have a plan, I'm going to personally kick your ass." He took the opportunity to force Sean out of the room, slamming the door in his face.

Chapter 5
Sean

Of course he wasn't going to stay. Sitting around and training while Gem had all the fun only to get the object he was training with taken away didn't sound like a good time to say the least. That annoying prick was just going to let it happen. *Who answers the door without a shirt on?* He thought to himself, sitting in his room waiting for Tirin to show up. He couldn't focus on that for too long. He had to figure out a plan before Tirin noticed he lied.

Getting past the guards was relatively easy. All a person had to do was create some kind of distraction. It was catching up to Gem's squad that would be difficult. With enough effort they could make it work, he was positive. He unfolded the written coordinates for the Neutral object and studied them closer. He thought maybe if he could figure out the general area it was located in, it might be easier to find a faster way there.

The longer he stared at it, the more something about the numbers seemed off to him. He studied the numbers. They didn't seem like normal numbers to him. His thoughts were interrupted by Tirin knocking on the door. Sean answered, glad to see Tirin fully clothed. He gestured for him to come in and shut the door behind him.

"What's the plan?"

Sean rolled his eyes. "Last time I explained a plan to you, I ended up having to explain it four times and even then you didn't stick to it. Do me a favor and just follow my lead this time."

"The last time I followed your lead, you ended up bound to the Sepratain object."

"Look, we don't have time for your attitude this time around. Every minute we waste here, the further the VAA gets to the Neutral object."

"I don't see why that's a bad thing. As much as I don't trust them, why waste our energy trying to catch up to them just to unbind you either way?"

Sean took a moment to gather his thoughts. Truthfully he never really trusted the VAA, but he trusted Gem. Something about unbinding the object felt wrong. Whether it was meant to be or not, it was *his* now, and he felt inclined to keep it. Then what? Go off the grid or escape on the run forever with one of the most powerful objects in Vermillia? That didn't matter to him. The Neutral object would most likely require someone with Necrotanian Object power to acquire, meaning if he wanted to find it and keep it from the VAA he'd need Tirin's help. Even then, Tirin would never agree to letting him keep it.

"I don't trust them with the object. What do you think they'll do about us once I'm not bound to their target? You want to risk that kind of punishment?"

Tirin tilted his head for a moment. "I don't trust the VAA as far as I can throw them either, but Gem got you into the mission. I'm sure she could keep you out of trouble. Unless you escape now. You do realize that if we do this, there is no doubt they will seek us out again."

"I'm willing to take that chance. I can't just rely on the hope that Gem can bail me out. She's gone through enough because of me already. And what about Antic? If we stay here, we're just sitting ducks waiting for his wave of anger to rain on our parade."

"Ok, riddle me this genius. How do you plan on getting to the object first when they have a head start?"

Sean looked down at the coordinates. "Tell me, does this not look strange to you?" He handed the paper to Tirin.

"The coordinates? It's just a bunch of numbers." Tirin furrowed his brow trying to understand what Sean was getting at.

"I think they're wrong."

"What do you mean by wrong?"

"Doesn't this paper look different than before?" He noticed the ruffer edges and the slightly off handwriting. "Here, write the exact same line underneath it." He handed Tirin a pen.

"Why? What's that supposed to prove?" He raised an eyebrow.

"Just do it."

Reluctantly, Tirin wrote the same coordinates underneath the first set. Sean's eyes grew wide. "I knew it!"

"What?"

"This isn't the same paper. Don't you get it? What exactly happened while I was unconscious?"

Tirin gave him a confused look. "Antic picked you up and started to walk away before running into the VAA who I sort of led to us in an effort to save the situation. Long story short, I ended up having to carry you the entire way to headquarters. What does any of that have to do with the coordinates?"

"Exactly." Sean decided to ignore the last part of that story. His face lit up. "Antic picked me up, and look," He compared the two lines of coordinates. "The handwriting is different."

Tirin crossed his arms. "Are you suggesting that Antic switched the coordinates while you were unconscious?"

"It makes sense doesn't it?"

He took another long look at the numbers. "You really think he anticipated not being able to capture you?"

"I know he did. He's a lot smarter than you think. The Sepratain trials are based on intelligence and he had to get first place in order to become the next heir. Besides," his gaze drifted, "I know him. He always has a backup plan."

"You do realize that means Gem's heading to the wrong place, and Antic has the real coordinates." Originally Tirin seemed hesitant about it, but now, Sean read his energy without even thinking. He was confident. Determined.

"The only problem now is if either of us remember the real coordinates." He thought hard about the numbers, trying to recall even just a single part of them. He sighed when he couldn't come up with anything.

Tirin looked at him like he was stupid. "That's easy. I can check the GPS history. We can just plug them in again."

Sean perked up. "Perfect."

"You seem a little too excited for someone who is being hunted by the heir to the Sepratain object." Tirin remarked. Sean could've sworn he saw a small hint of a smile at the corners of his lips.

He poked at his chest. "Some of us don't enjoy being cooped up in a headquarters building while lives are at stake. My life in particular." He grabbed his bag and pocketed the fake coordinates.

"And some of us like some relaxing time between missions, but apparently that's too much to ask for."

"How can anyone relax at a time like this?"

Tirin rolled his eyes. "It's simple. Just tell your brain to shut up."

Yeah, Sean thought, *because quieting an active mind is so simple.*

***

As anticipated it wasn't hard to escape. They weren't in a prison, just a large facility building that they weren't allowed to leave. In this case, Sean was grateful the VAA didn't exactly know how to properly guard against object attacks yet. They were from the normal continent after all. Tirin was able to summon a small Necrotanian creature as a distraction and they just walked right out after disabling the cameras which Sean used as target practice for his new object abilities.

The coordinates turned out to be closer to headquarters than the Vermillia's center line. The GPS read only a day's walk. It still wouldn't be easy with the most annoying person in the world right next to him the entire way, but Sean was starting to recognize something different in Tirin. Some kind of shift in his emotional reading. It wasn't any kind of care by any means, but it was lighthearted. Like he didn't want to punch him all the time anymore.

"Cut it out." Tirin's voice broke his thoughts.

"What?"

"You only get that look on your face when you're trying to read me."

Sean rolled his eyes as he walked along the narrow dirt path. "I do not have a 'look'."

Tirin let out a small huff of laughter. "You absolutely do. It's like when you're thinking except you also stare at me." Tirin furrowed his brows and brought a hand up to his chin, clearly trying to imitate Sean's thinking face.

Sean couldn't help but laugh at the childlike action. "That is NOT what I look like."

"Want to bet on that? Next time I catch you, I'll take a picture to prove it."

Sean stared at him for a moment with a bewilderment. *Is he smiling?* At first he thought he had to be imagining it because the only face Tirin ever made was brooding annoyance.

After a small pause in conversation, Tirin chuckled. "Don't get used to it."

Sean grew a smile of his own. "It looks good on you, you know."

"If you say so."

Chapter 6
Tirin

Alright, alright. Sean had been through a lot, and Tirin knew that. He figured if he was to expect anything from him, he would have to cut him some slack, even if that meant only for a moment. Maybe the annoying moron was growing on him, just a little. No harm in admitting that to himself, as long as no one knew about it. Besides, he had to admit it was hard not letting himself smile at least every once in a while. If they were going to be working together for who knows how long, Sean would have to see it eventually.

It was just pure luck that his reaction was also perfect. At the very least he expected to be teased about it forever, but all he did was smile. That stupid smile.

"It looks good on you, you know." He said through his grin.

Tirin looked away for a moment at the surrounding trees. "If you say so."

"I mean it. You should smile more often." He nudged him with his elbow.

"And then what? Become an emotional mess like you?" Just the thought of it made him sick.

"I am not a mess. Even if I was so what? What's wrong with emotions? They're part of being human." Sean looked at him genuinely.

"Emotions are vulnerable. No one deserves the right to know me that way." It was a simple concept really. Emotions could be a strength, but more often than not they were a weakness. Something that could be manipulated.

"And what would someone have to do to earn that right?" Sean's smile grew.

Immediately Tirin recognized his thought process. "In your dreams. If I open up to anyone, there's no way it'll be you."

Sean sighed. "Why not? Are you afraid of me or something." He raised an eyebrow.

Tirin paused for a moment. *Why not?* Sean annoyed him a lot sure, but it wasn't like he could have any capacity to manipulate anyone. He was far too emotional himself to even dream of pulling that off. Of course now he had some kind of expectation that Tirin would always be a stone wall. He decided breaking that persona could work against him at some point in the future. "Of course I'm not afraid of you. I could kick your ass easily."

Sean chuckled. "Exactly. If I tried anything you wouldn't let it slide so what's the harm in just letting your guard down every once in a while?"

Tirin sighed. "You're pushing your luck. It was just one smile. Isn't that enough for you?"

Sean smirked. "I won't tell anyone I saw it."

"Even if you did, they'd never believe you." He brushed it off, but just like that he felt the corners of his lips threaten to smile again. Since when was it this easy to get to him?

Sean groaned. "Can we take a break now? We've been walking for hours."

"You're such a lightweight."

Sean stopped in his tracks and chose a fallen tree trunk to sit on. "Maybe, but you don't seem to mind it as much as you say you do."

Tirin grit his teeth. "I told you not to read me."

Sean put his hands up defensively. "I didn't. It's just obvious."

He shot him a glare. "What do you mean obvious?"

"You haven't yelled at me, or even threatened me for the past few hours. That's a new record for you."

"So what? It doesn't mean anything." He crossed his arms.

Sean continued that small insignificant laugh. "What are you, a teenager? No one's going to care if you don't feel like punching me every time we talk."

"I do."

"Why? Why are you so set on being so closed off?"

Tirin couldn't let this happen. Not again. There was only one way to stop Sean from trying to pry into him and he would do anything to make it stop. "Maybe I don't want to associate myself with lesser people."

Sean scoffed. "You don't actually believe that. Just because I can't control a new object?"

"Yes, I do." He spoke firmly, without hesitation. He had to make it clear. "You're weak Sean. You got us into this mess, you failed the mission, you got disqualified in the Necrotanian trials. You're a failure and I don't get close to people like you."

Sean's entire demeanor changed. His eyes fell to the ground and he looked away from him. "That's not true..."

There was that look again. That same look that made Tirin's chest clench when he'd pretended to take Antic's deal. His eyes were almost begging. That was why he couldn't open up to him. The more he cared about someone, the more it eventually hurt. He had to end it before it got any worse. "Yes it is. After this is over our deal still stands."

Sean looked into his eyes desperately. "You don't mean that."

"We'll go our separate ways." He'd be lying to himself if he didn't admit that it somehow hurt to say, but it was for the best he thought. Yet he couldn't understand why Sean wasn't arguing with him. Normally when he insulted him he'd shoot something back and then Tirin could just blame it on the moment, but not this time. Sean grew quiet and that look in his eyes remained. He cursed himself for letting his guard down. To him, pain was the price of growing close to someone, and it wasn't worth the risk. Not anymore. Not after her.

"So maybe I am weak," to his surprise, Sean spoke, "and maybe I've made a lot of mistakes recently. I just don't understand why that means we have to hate each other." He paused for a moment, his hands gripping the log underneath him. He closed his eyes tightly. "Can't we just start over?"

This worked before, Tirin thought. *Why isn't it working now?* He couldn't bring himself to meet his eyes.

Sean opened his eyes and took a deep breath. "Ok. So you're not ready." He stood and dusted off his hands. "But when you are, I'm here."

Tirin looked away. "Don't count on it."

"I might not be the strongest, but I'm not giving up on you."

He scoffed. "If you're set on wasting your time, then be my guest."

Sean started walking again, this time he passed Tirin. For the First time in the entire trip, he was leading the way. He'd never seen him so determined. He had just been calling him weak and yet, there he was, acting as if he wasn't affected by any of his insults.

***

They walked in absolute silence for a few more hours until eventually they came upon a small town called Tendral. Unfortunately, Tirin knew of the town. Out of the few times he had been across Seprati's border, he'd visited Tendral to see an old friend. At least that's what he considered her now. She might not have considered it that way, but he could only hope he wouldn't have to find out how she saw their old relationship. It was risky stopping in a Sepratian town this far from the centerline. Not just because Tirin was in fact the fourth heir to the Necrotanian object, but also because by now their faces were all over the news. Someone was bound to recognize and report them to Antic and the forces.

Of course none of that mattered to Sean who had complained about being hungry for the past hour since they'd run out of their snacking supply. At least he was talking to him again, but at that point Tirin wondered if he actually preferred the animosity after all. After some convincing, they agreed to stop at the smallest gas station outside of town just long enough to get some supplies. They would get in, and get out. No time for messing around. At least that's how Tirin thought it would go, until he saw an annoyingly familiar car parked outside the store. Just his luck. As they got closer he hesitated.

"I'm going to stay out here and keep watch." He insisted as they got closer.

Sean nodded and made his way into the gas station. Tirin leaned on the wall outside, eyes fixed on the familiar car. The long outdated white paint job wasn't a pretty sight. It had gotten even more beat up then when he last saw it. Truthfully it could've been any car that just happened to also have that pink sticker on the back, but the possibility was enough to make him on edge. A large dent on the front of the car suggested an accident, but Tirin knew her better than that. She was a bit of a road rager, and out of all the "accidents" she had been in, most of them were her own fault. He tapped a finger on the side of his jeans, wondering how much longer he'd have to hope she wouldn't come out before Sean. He took a deep breath and tried to keep himself collected. It was no use. He never struggled with his own mind too much but at that moment he found himself going through what he might say to her if she showed up.

He tried to focus on anything other than the memory of their last interaction. The way she'd yelled at him just as he'd decided he might actually get over his commitment issues. An obvious mistake on his part. She was anything but a patient person. He closed his eyes for a moment, listening listened to the sounds around him. The light breeze. The distant chirping of the birds. Then, the opening of the door.

"Tirin..." Sean's voice.

"I told you to—" He stopped dead as he opened his eyes to meet with the girl he had been dreading seeing.

"She insisted..." Sean said weakly.

"I told him I'd let both of you go if *you* talked to me." She said, her expression just as firm and stubborn as it had been when they last spoke a year ago.

Tirin sighed. "Ok. You're talking to me. Are we done?"

"No we're not *done*. You owe me some answers." She crossed her arms. Tirin observed her. Not much had changed. She still had the same sense of style, a sort of academic look. The same jet black hair that always fell straight over her shoulders. The only real difference was the way she was looking at him like she wanted to punch him.

Sean looked between the two of them. He held up a shaky hand, offering his power to Tirin, presumably to keep him peaceful. He shook his head. He'd gotten himself into this mess, now he had to get himself out.

"Alright. Ask your questions."

She grit her teeth. "Because that's all you're here for isn't it? You don't even care to say hi. You were just going to leave."

Tirin rolled his eyes. "I'm not here for you Jordan. I'm here for him." He gestured to Sean. Jordan looked between them. She winced at his words.

"How long will you keep *this one* on a string?" She looked at Sean coldly. "Don't get used to him. He doesn't hang around for long."

Sean put up his hands in defense. "No, we're not like *that.*"

"Quite the opposite actually." Tirin said.

"So you're a criminal now? Is that how you dealt with our break up?" She spat.

"What break up? We weren't a thing."

"What were we then?"

Tirin paused, thinking on the question. It's not like he didn't like her, he just wasn't into what she wanted. She'd convinced him that maybe he could want something like that, but it was short lived after she bit his head off the night. She was a moment in time and nothing more. A reflection of something he didn't want in his life. *A relationship.* An all out expectation of what it means to be vulnerable.

Sean shot him a look that said *you better shut up before we get reported.* Tirin grit his teeth.

"What can I offer you in return for your silence?" The sentence came out forced through the gaps in his teeth.

"Fuck you. *Fuck you.*"

He scoffed. "No thanks."

"Dam you and your fucking jokes. That's what all of this is to you isn't it? A fucking joke."

He rolled his eyes. "If you're going to report us anyway, I see no point in continuing this interaction."

She winced. "Was it at least good?"

Tirin raked his brain for the memories from a year ago to try and remember anything about the intimacy. He shrugged. "Mediocre at best." That part at least was the truth. It had taken him a long time to realize he might've not even been into girls in the first place. That didn't mean he never saw her as more than a companion whether he wanted to admit it or not.

"I did some thinking, you know. You're an asshole because you're a coward."

"You thinking? that's rare."

"You're just afraid. Afraid it'll be just like your dad and that fucking dog."

Tirin's fist instantly balled. "This isn't about that."

"It was always about that. You want to keep being a coward and not facing it, fine. Just don't go fucking around with people to make yourself feel better anymore. Clearly it hasn't worked."

Sean stood between them. He gave Tirin *that* look. Those eyes that peered into him as he read his emotional state. He shot him a glare. "Quit looking at me like that."

Sean sighed. "Let's just go." He turned towards Jordan, with what Tirin thought might be sympathy. "Look, I'm sorry for whatever happened, but it's really important that you don't rat us out. If we get caught my own life is on the line. They'll kill me. Don't do it for him. Do it for the sake of not being the reason I die."

Jorden sighed and uncrossed her arms. "You seem like a nice guy. What's got you tangled up with that asshole?"

"It's a long story."

"Trust me it's purely situational." Tirin added bitterly. Sean looked at the ground, his eyes telling a story of their own.

"I know that look. Don't judge your worth based on what someone else thinks of you." Jorden put a hand on his shoulder.

He offered her a weak smile. "Thanks."

"I won't report you." She turned to Tirin. "This has nothing to do with you."

He turned away, looking for an escape. Out of all the ways that conversation could've gone, he was pretty sure that was one of the worst outcomes. After all that he felt something. Something he wasn't used to. *Guilt.*

Chapter 7
Sean

Jorden knew things about Tirin. Things that Sean didn't know. It didn't matter what their relationship had been. All Sean could think about was how much Tirin had clearly trusted the girl, and how he didn't trust him. As they continued walking through the rocky roads outside of Tendral, Sean found himself lost in his own thoughts again. *What does she have that I don't?* That emotion he'd sensed in Tirin at the gas station, that was real. A stream of gray clouds through the black smoke of his usual aura. The way he insisted that their partnership was "purely situational" made his gut twist in knots. Maybe their relationship had started out that way, but he thought they had grown on each other. Now he was realizing that maybe Tirin had just grown on him, and not the other way around. He was convinced it was foolish to think anything else.

He stared at the back of his head as they walked, desperately wishing he could catch even just a glimpse of what went on in his mind. He thought back to what Jordan said. *How long are you going to keep this one on a string?* He shifted uncomfortably. All those times Tirin had been just a little bit nicer, *was it even real?* As if things couldn't get any worse between them, they didn't speak for hours. The silence practically haunted Sean. He hated being trapped in his mind. He felt lost and out of control.

Finally they stopped for a break behind a few bushes off the road they had been walking on. Tirin handed Sean a water bottle, not saying a single word. Sean couldn't take it anymore. He looked into his eyes clutching his pendant. Tirin's aura was a mess of clouds swirling, just as confusing as his own feelings. He felt a lump forming in his throat.

"Stop looking at me like that." Tirin said.

"Like what?" Sean's voice came out unintentionally weak.

"Like you could burst into tears at any moment."

Sean looked away as he heard him speak. "How am I supposed to look at you?"

"I don't know, just not like that."

Sean took a sip of the water he was given and tried to keep himself collected.

Tirin continued, "It's making me sick."

Sean clutched the water bottle tighter. "I *always* make you sick don't I? What's the difference?"

Tirin hesitated. "You don't always make me sick..."

Sean looked at him as he paused. Whatever he was about to say, he'd decided it wasn't real. It couldn't be real. Tirin hated him, and Sean felt as if that was the way it would alwyas be. "Then why act like it? You don't have to lie to me. I'll get over it..."

"I'm not lying—"

"Yes you are. I get it, you hate me. I've had enough of this game, just stop."

Tirin's eyes poured into him. "I thought you said you wouldn't give up on me."

Sean scoffed. "I don't see the point if our relationship is 'purely situational'."

Tirin stepped closer, his presence unwavering. "You know it's more than that."

"Do I know that? When have you ever admitted that to me? You're such a—"

"I'm admitting it now." He said sharply. "I don't hate you. I hate you're haunting silence more than you annoying me. Just... talk to me now. Please."

Sean met his gaze, searching his eyes. "What about Jorden? Am I going to end up like her to you?"

"Jorden was never like you."

"Then tell me what makes her different? You clearly trusted her and not me."

Tirin sighed, running a hand through his hair. "Jorden was a fling. That was all it was ever supposed to be. Then she got too close... She wanted more than I could give her. I left. Maybe it was a bit sudden to her, but you can see why right? She's headstrong. She has the patience of a dam hummingbird. It wouldn't have been an easy conversation."

"So you just left her like you want to leave me."

"You're different Sean..."

"Different how? From the moment we started the mission we agreed we'd do what we have to do, then separate. Is it so hard to think that maybe I don't want that anymore?"

Tirin let the silence grow. He averted his gaze. Sean answered for him. "That's what I thought. When this is over you can leave. Just don't pretend like you won't." He sealed his water bottle and walked back out of the bushes. He was done talking. He was done believing that Tirin would actually care. Even when the thought of it pained him physically, he pushed it down. The faster they got this job done, the faster he could get away from him. Maybe then the pain would go away.

***

Sean walked ahead of Tirin for a while before realizing that Tirin had the GPS and he didn't know where to go. He let him walk ahead and lagged behind as usual. Again the silence grew for hours, but this time Sean's mind was quiet. He'd said what he wanted to. He'd made his peace with the situation. He looked up at the clouds between the trees every now and then, tracing out the shapes as a means to keep himself relaxed. First a small butterfly, then a Sepratain creature, then a dragon.

Eventually he started to think he should've tried to become an artist. He traced a heart, then a person, then a dark cloud. No wait, that was a rain cloud. He looked ahead at Tirin who was reading the GPS signals. The cloud was larger than he thought as he looked at the darkness ahead. He caught up to him.

"A storm?"

"A big one." Tirin answered.

"Is it too late to go around it?"

"We'll be lucky if we get moderately soaked. Honestly, we might just have to hunker down for the night here."

Sean nodded. They found a decent spot to set up the tent and began preparing to keep things in place and as dry as they could. They sacrificed a sleeping bag to cover their important belongings. Tirin set up the tent under a large tree, but they both knew that wouldn't stop them from eventually getting wet. As they climbed into the tent for the night, the two prepared for the worst. Sean, without his sacrificed sleeping bag, curled up into his jacket against the wall of the tent. He forced himself to relax as he heard the distant rumbling of thunder.

As usual Tirin stayed on the opposite side of the small tent, as far as possible from Sean, but this time he was facing him. At first it made him uncomfortable to think that Tirin's eyes might be on his back so he turned to face him as well. Of course that only made it worse as they just ended up meeting eyes every now and then. The rain finally started, thankfully giving Sean something else to focus on other than the awkward positioning. He focused on the light patter of the rain hitting the tent and the rumbling of thunder, still far off in the distance. There was something calming about the constant sound. It made his eyes feel heavier.

Tirin met his gaze again. There was something else in his eyes. He knew he shouldn't have, but he read him. His aura read like a calm stream of gray clouds. To his surprise, there was no smoke. No black puffs of something angry surrounding him. For the first time, Tirin wasn't even a little annoyed, and by the look of it, he wasn't trying to hide it either. He nodded and looked away, as if acknowledging Sean's reading.

Sean spoke quietly through the sounds of the light rain. "Are you just tired, or is there something you want to say to me?"

Tirin kept his gaze away. "I don't want to be close to you." His voice came out flat.

Sean raised an eyebrow. "You don't want to, or you're afraid to?" He saw him visibly hesitate. "You already let me read you. Lie to me all you want but I know how you're feeling."

"Whether I want to be close to you or not doesn't matter, it just shouldn't happen."

"Why not? What's wrong with it?"

"Because being close to people means leaving yourself open for weakness." He still wouldn't meet his eyes.

"Do you really think I'd try to hurt you that badly?"

"It doesn't matter what I think. I have to avoid that chance altogether."

Sean shifted a bit closer. "Look, I don't know what I have to do to convince you that I'm trustworthy, but I'll do it."

Tirin huffed. "That's because you're stupid. You trust people too easily. How do you know I won't hurt you if you open up to me?"

Sean rolled his eyes. "I don't know if you'll hurt me or not, but it's worth the risk if it means I could gain a friendship from it."

"Yeah, because that seemed to go really well with Antic."

Sean felt a familiar pain in his chest. "That wasn't my fault."

"Antic doesn't seem to think that." The rain outside grew stronger as he spoke. Flashes of lightning were finally more visible through the tent but the thunder was still distant.

"You don't even know what happened."

"Maybe I don't but I know what came after it. That tells me all I need to know. You're stupid enough to risk a friendship with someone like that."

"Ok. Maybe I am stupid. Fine." Sean said. He clutched his jacket, feeling a chill pass through the tent from the wind picking up outside.

Tirin's aura changed. The gray clouds swirled around him for a moment. He met his eyes again. "That doesn't mean I want you to leave. It's just the way it has to be."

"It doesn't have to be anything. You chose the way it ends up." He begged him for an ounce of understanding.

"After everything I've done to you, why do you insist on trying to break me open?" Sean hesitated. He didn't understand it himself. Tirin spoke for him. "Is it some form of pity? Do you think I'm lonely or something and you just have to save me?"

The heavier the sounds of the rain outside got, the more chaotic Sean's mind seemed to get. He stayed silent, trying to process it all.

Again Tirin spoke. "That's what it is isn't it. You've got some superhero complex and you think I'm weak enough to play into it." Despite everything he said, there still wasn't an ounce of dark smoke in his aura. It was like he kept trying to force it out through the swirl of gray clouds, but the smoke just wouldn't come. "Is that the real reason why you joined the VAA? You wanted a chance to *save* Antic?"

"You want to know what happened don't you? You want to know so badly that you just have to use it against me so I'll have no choice but to tell you. Why? Do you think it'll make me less than you?" Sean spat. Lighting flashed outside and a loud rumble followed it.

Tirin hesitated. His aura settled. He looked away, seemingly realizing something. Sean's mind settled and then suddenly crashed as the answer came into view like a spinning compass that stopped directly on north. "You're jealous…"

"Do you have to make it sound like I care about you?" Sean made a mental note of how he didn't deny the statement. The pouring rain seemed to settle a bit.

Sean sighed, understanding what he had to do to fix the mess of emotions. "I'll tell you what happened."

Tirin just stared at him silently, expecting something more.

"Antic and I were very close friends a few years ago. And when I say close, I mean it. To the point where my sister asked me if I was gay for him." Sean paused, recalling the exchange.

"And?"

"And I told her I was gay, but not for him." He gave a small sigh. "Looking back, I should've recognized all the signs. We joked about being together a lot. We'd stay up late and watch the stars. Until it all came crashing down." He ran a hand through his hair. "I knew he had feelings for me and I just kept playing along so I wouldn't lose him. I know it wasn't right and I should've told him sooner but I just couldn't face the reality of it."

Tirin's eyes dug into his soul. "He wanted to be with you."

"Yes, and I didn't want that with him." He felt a familiar ache in his chest. "And instead of just accepting it and moving on, he hated me, going on and on about how much I led him on and hurt him. So I cut ties with him. He gave me no choice. The next time I heard of him, he was heir to the Sepratain object. Gem and I both knew taking the mission with the VAA would be risky, but we agreed if anyone could talk sense into him when the time came for it, it would be me. Of course none of that mattered when I screwed everything up and found myself bound to the object."

Tirin stayed silent, his expression unreadable.

"Because that's just who I am. I mess everything up and I push everyone out of my life that's worth having. I'm sorry I got you into this mess." Another moment of silence passed. "If you're going to leave me, just do it now before I get any more hope that things might be different this time..." The rain outside dulled to the quiet patter and distant rumbling it was before. Sean met his eyes. "Just say something... please..."

Tirin's eyes softened. "I don't want to leave." He searched his gaze, sure he would catch him in a lie, but he didn't. Tirin shifted closer to him. "I mean it."

"There's no way in hell I believe that..." Sean started weakly.

Tirin again shifted closer, now only inches away. "If you don't trust my words then-" He gently wrapped his arms around him. Sean froze, his heart wanting to let go but his mind still denying it. Until he heard three words Tirin said. Three simple words that somehow could fix everything.

"*I'm sorry, Sean.*"

Chapter 8
Tirin

He woke to Sean shifting, his body practically pressed up against him. He didn't mind. After all, Sean had sacrificed his sleeping bag for their supplies in the storm the night before. *Last night*, He thought to himself as the memory of what was said flooded his mind. Maybe it was a stupid decision. Maybe it would all come crashing down soon, but at that moment, he didn't care. He'd have to deal with that when it happened.

Somehow the emotional idiot had wormed his way closer to him. Part of him hated it. It bothered him to his very core. Another part of him wanted to just let it be. If they could be friends, would it make the journey easier? It was tiring to keep up the fight all the time. This way he could preserve that energy for more important things, like summoning his object power.

The light of the morning sunrise creeped in through the tent's opening. He hesitated. They'd have to get back to the mission, but he didn't want to leave the moment of peace. With all the complicated stuff they were heading towards, it wasn't surprising that he wanted to keep all of that stuff away, just a little bit longer. Even worse, it meant he'd have to wake Sean from the peaceful state of sleep. He hadn't slept that well the entire journey, Tirin knew that. He was an emotional person, and Tirin was sure all that emotion must've been exhausting. Still, he knew there were people after them. He'd have to wake him eventually.

He gently patted his side. "Hey, wake up."

Sean furrowed his brow, stirring slightly. "Hm?" He hummed a sleepy response.

The sound made Tirin's chest tighten. "We have to keep moving." He nudged him a few times. Sean stirred again, peaking open his eyes. He looked up at him, not fully processing his surroundings. "Come on moron."

Sean leaned his head against him. "Just a little longer."

Tirin froze up a bit. "Sean, we have to get to the object before anyone else does."

Sean groaned before rubbing his eyes gently. He must've woken himself up a bit more because he looked up at Tirin like he'd seen a ghost.

Tirin chuckled. "Relax. You act like I'm going to bite you or something."

Sean shifted awkwardly. "Is the stuff ok? It was in the storm all night."

Tirin sat up. He had forgotten about the stuff they'd covered in Sean's sleeping bag to protect against the heavy rain. He unzipped the tent, the dewy smell of the humid morning hitting him like a wave. He got out of the tent and stretched for a moment before uncovering the two back-packs they had wrapped the sleeping bag over. It seemed like the idea had worked for the most part. Most of the stuff was mildly damp but it wasn't unsalvageable.

"Seems ok to me."

Sean made his way out of the tent and shuffled through his bag. "Could be worse I guess."

Tirin started breaking down the tent. He looked over at Sean who stood awkwardly watching. After he finished putting away the tent he sighed. "Ok, what's wrong?"

Sean hesitated. "What do you mean?"

"Why are you being so quiet? You're usually the morning person."

"I'm just tired."

Tirin could see through that lie from a million miles away. He decided it wasn't important. Just because Sean had opened up to him the night before, didn't mean he expected him to always be completely up front with him. He pulled out the GPS and began walking along the small dirt path they had been following. Sean walked behind as usual. As quiet as he was, Tirin knew he was probably overthinking everything that happened the night before. That was just the type of person Tirin had come to know him as. He slowed his walking pace, walking alongside him now. If he didn't want to talk about it, the Tirin would show him it was ok in other ways. Physical gestures always made better sense to him anyways.

After a couple minutes, Tirin noticed the way Sean visibly relaxed. He would look over with a small smile every now and again. He breathed a silent sigh of relief, seeing him relax. With everything they were going through, he felt Sean deserved that much.

***

After a few hours, they entered a small town at the coastal border of Seprati. Unlike Tendral, Kegh was an even smaller town. There were very few people out and about, and almost every shop seemed empty or on the verge of closing down. The dirt path turned into a rocky street. Rocky might be an understatement. The road was quite literally put together by large stones buried into the ground. At the very end of the road stood a Neutralist temple. Easily identifiable by its triangular shape and the usage of gray color.

Of course this temple wasn't beaming with floating lanterns or even any sort of statues along the steps. It was run down and overlooked. The vegetation had grown around it and almost encapsulated the entrance. The GPS beeped as they reached the steps. That was it. If the Neutral object was real, it would be in that temple. The pair stopped as they reached the entrance.

"Whatever is in there, it's not going to be good." Tirin concluded, remembering the warning they had been given by Ira.

"Before we go in, I need to ask you something." Sean turned to face him.

"What is it?"

"Did you mean what you said last night?"

Tirin let a small smile pull at the corners of his lips. "Seriously?"

Sean looked away embarrassed. "I just want to make sure."

Tirin nudged his shoulder. "Of course I meant it."

"What happens if this isn't what we want it to be?" He met his eyes, a worried look in them. "Are you still going to stay with me?"

Tirin softened his gaze. "We'll figure it out." He started clearing away some of the vines around the entrance. "I mean, this is a Neutralist temple. That has to be a good sign."

Sean reached a hand out to the large handle of the double doors. "It can't be that simple. Why wouldn't someone else have found the object by now if it was in here?"

"Maybe no one else has come in here with the Sepratain or Necrotanian object."

Sean sighed. Tirin knew he was right. There was no way it was going to be that easy. The warning had said the object was protected heavily. He braced himself as Sean pushed open the doors. "There's no going back now."

Chapter 9
Sean

The large wooden doors swung open with a loud creek. At first nothing was visible in the pitch black of the temple. Sean pulled out a small flashlight. The entryway was spacious. It was similar to the temple in the center line, but smaller. There were paintings along the walls and pillars on either side of the building. Sean felt something churn in his stomach at the emptiness of the space. As they stepped into the room, they left the door open behind them, not wanting to shut out the source of light. They walked along the large hall looking at the various paintings. They each depicted some sort of older superior, but they were different from the ones at Ira's temple. They were much older paintings, collecting dust in the abandoned temple.

Sean heard the voice of what sounded like a little boy coming from the back area of the temple. He shined his flashlight in that direction but saw nothing.

"Did you hear that?"

Tirin nodded, making sure to check behind them. The voice grew a bit louder. Sean was able to make out some of the words. *Please, he needs help.*

"Hello?" Sean walked towards the back of the room where the voice was coming from. Then the whimper of a puppy encoded along the empty hall. Again the voice came. *Please! Rowdy didn't do anything wrong!*

Tirin froze, wide eyed. "Rowdy." He muttered. The temple door suddenly slammed shut behind them. The paintings on the walls began to glow, dimly lighting the space. A young boy sat in the center of the room next to a dog who had been severely injured. The young boy's image was still, frozen in time. Tirin stepped closer, not saying a single word. Sean's breathing accelerated, a sense of adrenaline spiking in him.

Tirin stood next to the boy. Sean's eyes drifted between the dark haired boy and Tirin. "Wait a minute..." The pieces collided together in his mind. "Is that you?"

Tirin reached out to the image of the boy who was crying on his knees next to the puppy. His hands phased through the image, as if it was a projection. "Close your eyes." He said urgently.

"What?"

"Close your eyes Sean." He said, the little boy started to move. Tears flooded his eyes. He petted the puppy's face, gently caressing its snout. *It's going to be ok, Rowdy.*

"I said close your eyes." Tirin demanded.

Sean understood. It felt like something he wasn't supposed to be seeing. Some kind of invasion of privacy. As much as he wanted to see, he forced his eyes shut. Still he heard the voices. Another voice came through. The voice of an older man. *This is what happens. This is why we do not get attached to things.*

The boy sobbed. *Please father, help him.*

What has he done for you but cause trouble? You need to learn to keep your emotions in line if you're ever going to be something significant. The father said sternly.

Sean flinched as he heard a loud whimper from the puppy again followed by the cry of the boy. *Stop it, please!*

That pain you feel, that is what you need to rely on. You can either use it as power or you can keep it away from you. Either way, it always results in hurting. The older man said. The crying from the boy seemed to die down. Sean heard the shuffling of clothes like an embrace.

I'm sorry. It won't happen again. The boy said defeated.

It's ok Tirin. That's just the way it has to be. You understand, right?

Yes.

After a moment, the voices and the sounds died down to nothing. Sean peaked open his eyes to see Tirin sitting on the ground staring at the spot where the image of the boy had been. There was nothing else anymore. It was just him in the middle of the empty temple.

Sean walked over to him without saying a word. He opened his mouth to speak, but he found that words didn't quite fit the moment. He placed a hand on his shoulder lightly. Tirin didn't resist or back away. He didn't say anything, he just sat there for a few long moments, staring down at the ground.

Suddenly, a door in the back of the room swung open with a creek. Another voice could be heard through the door. The voice of a girl this time. It felt familiar in some way.

"I don't want to go." Tirin said firmly.

"We have too. We don't have any other way out of here."

Tirin sighed, gripping his backpack straps. Sean understood him. After all this time with him, he knew Tirin hated being vulnerable. If this place was going to show the memories of his past, there was no telling just how unprotected he felt.

"I won't look. I won't even listen if you don't want me to." Sean gave his shoulder a light squeeze. If there was anyone who responded to touch better than words, it was him.

"No..." Tirin managed to say. He stood. "You should look... It might be important to the object..." He closed his eyes for a moment, taking a deep breath.

The girl's voice echoed through the building, the actual words she was saying undecipherable. Tirin met his eyes. Sean nodded. They continued through the door towards the sound. Sean stopped in his tracks at the image they saw. It was Gem. She was gripping Sean's shirt. He closed his eyes and took a deep breath, preparing himself for the memory. He knew the exact moment.

It doesn't belong to you. The teenage version of Gem spoke firm, a hint of anger surrounding her.

The younger version of himself clutched the pendant around his neck. *I-I'm sorry. I can't give it to you.*

Sean looked over at Tirin who was watching the interaction with a blank expression.

You don't even know how hard I worked for that. Gem spat, letting go of his shirt she had bundled in her fist.

It isn't my fault. You know dad didn't approve. He said sheepishly.

Gem sighed. *But you could've saved it. You could've waited to bind to it just a little longer until I got back.*

The real Sean clutched his pendant. He'd regretted that moment every day since it happened. Gem deserved the family heirloom way more than he did. He blamed himself for everything. It didn't matter that his father wouldn't have approved. He should've stood up for his sister. After all she'd done for him, he couldn't muster the courage.

Sean mouthed the words he knew his younger self would say. *I'm so sorry.* The younger Sean muttered, not able to meet Gem's eyes.

I can't believe he'd rather give it to a failure than a girl. She said under her breath as she walked away. Her image faded, leaving the younger image of Sean to deal with the aftermath.

Tirin placed a hand on Sean's shoulder. He could at least give him the same comfort he offered him.

****

They must've been in the temple for hours just watching each other's memories play out. They were shown every single worst moment of their lives until that point. There was no way to fully understand a person more than they were coming to understand each other. Sean saw all of Tirin's worst moments. The time his father got him a dog, only to teach him a lesson about attachments. It wasn't the last time his father would ruin or take away anything Tirin got too close to. The time he got picked on in junior high. The time he almost got arrested for fighting back. He even saw his full break up with Jordan. The way he'd almost let her in before she'd lost her patience with him. It was like he was watching Tirin's heart bear and open for everything it was.

Of course it wasn't just Tirin. Sean's memories were on full display, and he was forced to relive every single one of them. The time he was given the family object over Gem. The time he'd failed at presenting an important speech to his senior class. The time he'd been told he'd never be enough for any kind of object more powerful than his own. The time of his grandmother's passing, and how much he regretted not being there to say goodbye. Even every bad decision he'd made in his friendship with Antic. Watching it over again he was starting to realize the things he missed about Antic as a person. The way he had some kind of control over the things Sean was allowed to say or do around him. He couldn't face it. He'd pushed it so deep into his mind that he didn't know how to accept it. It all came crashing down on him. As shamed as he felt, it helped to have Tirin there. A constant presence of security, even through the harsh memories.

Then there were the memories they both shared. A familiar image projected in front of them. Sean on one side of the room, Tirin on the other. They had both summoned Necrotanian creatures during the trials. At that particular moment, their creatures had beaten each other evenly. They were down to the physical fight. Flashes of light blinded the room as they battled it out.

Tirin's voice came through the noise. *Just give up already. You know you can't beat me.*

Sean's image clenched his fists tighter. *Watch me.*

The real pair had sat themselves against the wall, knowing exactly how the outcome of the memory would play out. They exchanged glances.

Oh please, you've always been a failure. Don't get your hopes up now. Tirin's image said, the smirk on his face taunting.

Sean's image clashed with his again. *You don't have the right to say that.*

Oh really? Not even after I beat your sister in last year's trial? Get over yourself.

She was injured. It wasn't a fair fight. Sean winced, knowing exactly how his image would react to all the teasing. His reaction would be the downfall.

Tirin's image clashed with his once more, further taunting him. *Your whole family just can't stop failing, and you're the worst of them.*

Sean's image grunted as he eyed him dangerously. He charged at him filled with rage. At the right moment, Tirin's image stepped out of the way. Sean stood there stunned. He'd stepped out of bounce, disqualifying him from the trials. Just like that he'd failed again, and lost Tirin.

Tirin's image laughed as the bell sounded indicating the end of the match. *What a waste of a match.*

The images faded away, leaving the pair in the dim light of the temple. Sean felt Tirin's hand grab his own.

"I'm sorry..."

Sean let out a sigh. "I know."

Sean's voice came from the edge of the first large room they had walked into, muffled through another door. After everything they'd seen they knew where it ended. The last memory. They stood up and walked through the door, the room having an exceptionally tall ceiling. Sean's image glowed in front of them.

What are you doing? Tirin's voice.

Sean looked like he was in some kind of trance as the glowing image of the Sepratain object appeared in front of him. Without a physical form, it appeared as a glowing orb of light, fluctuating and bending the space around it.

Sean? Tirin's voice again. His image appeared a couple feet away from Sean's along with another. Antic.

Oh this is precious. He said in a sharp voice.

Tirin shouted at him. *Stay back.* His earring glowing, ready to summon his object's power.

I'm the heir to the Sepratain object. You think you've got a shot at beating me? you'll be lucky to leave with your life. Antic took a small step closer, testing the boundaries. *You won't be able to get him to move anyways.*

Sean's eyes widened as he watched the scene unfold. He didn't remember that part. He'd been in a trance in front of the object. He knew Tirin had saved him, but he didn't know how.

I'm guessing you've never been this close to an object this powerful before? Antic's image smirked at Tirin's image.

What does that matter? I can still kick your ass. He said, firm in his stance.

Look at him. He's not going to move. The object has its hold on him unfortunately. Antic's aura was fuming with smoke. Sean understood that he'd accepted something that made him enraged to his very core. He knew him well enough to tell how much anger he was suppressing.

What do you mean by that?

The object shows you what you want to see. And seeing as you've broken into the vault I assume you're both here to steal it.

Tirin's image shifted threateningly as Antic came closer.

You don't get it do you?

Get what?

Your friend is going to bind to it. Unfortunately that means I have to kill him.

Tirin tensed. *He wouldn't do that.*

How well do you know him? Trust me, he will. Sean grit his teeth. Tirin didn't know of their history before. At the time he couldn't really understand the depth of what Antic was implying.

Sean's image reached out a hand to the Object. Tirin's Image rushed over to him. *Don't do it Sean!*

He isn't going to listen to you. He wants to do it, so he will. It's that simple.

If that's true then why aren't you stepping in to stop him?

You don't know a thing do you?

Sean tensed realizing in that moment that Antic let him bind to the object on purpose. A stabbing pain of betrayal shot through his chest. He'd wanted him to bind to the object so that he could have the excuse to hurt him. Not just that but he wanted to do more than hurt him. He knew he'd have to kill him in order to get the object back.

Tirin's image grabbed onto Sean's arm, trying to shake him out of it. Sean's projection propelled into the object seemingly triggered by Tirin's intervention. A blinding light flashed through the room. The real Sean turned, meeting eyes with Tirin.

The silence between them grew but it was almost comfortable. After everything they'd seen, the deepest parts of each other on full display, there was some kind of unspoken trust between them. Still, the lingering pain rested on Sean's shoulders. Partially from what he'd been seeing and partially from the idea of Antic wanting him dead from the very beginning.

"I think that's the last of them." Tirin said with a relieved sigh.

"If that's true then where's the object?"

The Sepratain Object on Sean's wrist started to glow. He felt an odd tingling sensation where its power resided against his skin. The dim white glow casting a shadow onto his face. Another voice came. A distant, deep, male voice. One neither of them seemed to recognize. The image of an older man materialized in front of them. His features weren't relevant to the brightly shining object in front of him. They gray color to the glow, a clear indication of the Neutral object. A smaller figure appeared behind the man, seemingly a child.

The kid spoke. *Are you sure that will work? What if it makes things worse?*

The man replied, his voice ruff. *It has to work. Splitting the object in two is the only way.*

Sean and Tirin took a step closer, paying close attention to what looked like a memory from the Sepratain object itself. The man made a dramatic gesture with his arms and started chanting something in a language neither of them recognized. The Neutral object's glow flashed brighter and brighter until finally, the man made a sweeping motion and the object itself shattered in half. Sean and Tirin stood there, gaping mouthed as the pieces of the Neutral object took on their own separate colors. One a bright white, the other a dark black.

"You have to be kidding me..." Sean muttered as the images before them faded. The glow around the paintings in the temple faded, leaving the two in complete darkness.

"This whole time, the Sepratain and Necrotanian objects have both been just two parts of the Neutral object? That can't be right." He fished out his flashlight from his pocket.

The second he turned on the flashlight he saw Tirin's expression, then the black smoke coming from his aura. "Tirin?"

Tirin gripped his fists tightly by his sides. "All this way for nothing."

"It's ok. We can figure this out." Sean tried to say. He knew how pathetic it sounded but he didn't know what else to say.

"This is NOT ok Sean. That means we have to somehow steal the Necrotanian object and figure out how to merge the two objects back together, if that's even possible." His voice grew louder than before. He was losing himself and Sean knew it.

"Tirin..." Sean placed a hand gently on his shoulder, clutching his pendant. He pulled the power from his family heirloom through his body and out of his hand. He watched as the dark smoke in Tirin's aura started to dissipate. "... It *is* ok."

Chapter 10
Tirin

He took a deep breath. To him it felt like it had been a long time since he'd last felt Sean's calming ability. The familiar way it pulsed through his body, consuming all of his anger and washing it out of him made his shoulders fall. He sighed. "Thanks."

Sean nodded. "We're going to figure this out."He dropped his hand to his side. "I just don't know where to begin."

"It looks like we need the Necrotanian Object if we want to unbind you."

"Are you saying we have to combine the objects? That could go so wrong."

Tirin knew what he meant. Putting together the objects that had been apart for decades was a horrible idea. The objects decided who led the kingdom itself. The Neutralist movement was one thing, but changing the way the kingdom ran entirely was another. The whole system would have to change, and there was no doubt that change wouldn't come easy.

"There is no other option."

"There is..." Sean looked away sheepishly.

Tirin felt a pain in his chest. He'd gone all that time protecting him, and there was no way he'd let him turn himself in just to die. "That's off the table." He said, his voice firm. Sean met his gaze. Tirin tried to understand him. It was as if he didn't expect him to say that. After everything they'd gone through, he'd remind him till the end of the earth. "I'm not going to let you die Sean."

"You're forgetting that we have the world chasing us."

"I don't care." Sean's eyes were fixed on the ground. After everything Tirin had done to fuck him over, he owed it to him to keep him safe. He spoke softer, placing a hand on his shoulder. "Sean, look at me." He met his eyes. "I said I'm not letting you die. I mean it."

Sean reluctantly nodded.

"I know the Necrotanian heir. I met her and fought her in the trials, but she isn't going to just hand us the object."

"Of course not."

"It won't be easy to steal either. Not after we stole the Sepratain object. I bet they've tightened security. We'll be lucky if she hasn't performed the binding ceremony early."

"Then we won't steal it."

Tirin gripped his shoulder tighter. "I said I'm not letting you die."

Sean put his hands up defensively. "No, I mean, we'll force her to hand it over."

"How do you suppose we do that? I've already lost to her in the trials. As much as I want a rematch, I'm fourth in line. She won't give it up unless I beat her in battle for it."

"I've seen what you can do, and you've had more practice now.'

"Sean, you know I can't just challenge the heir without the trials. That's not how that works."

Sean smirked. "Think about it. Think about the person she is. Viera is a competitive person. you can use her arrogance. You just have to play your cards right and get her to challenge you legally."

"That's not going to work."

"Tirin, you're a persistent person. You know exactly how to push people's buttons. Just talk her up like you did me."

Tirin visibly tensed. He'd used Sean's weaknesses to manipulate him in the contest, but Sean was easier to read than Viera. She proved that the day they fought each other in the trials. "It's not going to be easy and it might not even work."

"If you won't let me go, then what choice do we have?"

That was it. That is what he had to do to protect him. If he had to beat the dam heir to the Necrotanian object to keep him alive, then he would. He took a long breath. He *would* keep him alive.

***

The walk from the temple was like the other times, absolutely silent at first, but this silence was different. It was comfortable. They'd seen a lot. They'd been through a lot. Tirin didn't think he'd ever be this comfortable around someone in his life, and yet there they were, walking side by side, nothing to say to each other, and nothing to be afraid of. After seeing the worst parts of Tirin, Sean stayed by his side. That meant more to him than Sean would ever know.

He found himself lost in his thoughts for once. Normally that kind of thing was reserved for Sean, but Tirin couldn't stop thinking about all he'd seen, and the way Sean had just accepted it all without question. Sean seemed lost in his own thoughts as usual. Tirin took the opportunity to observe him. There were things he found himself starting to see differently in him.

The way his hair fell along his face and behind his neck. The way his gray eyes reflected the light of the stars. The way his hands gripped the straps of his backpack as he walked. Then the way the straps shaped his chest. He closed his eyes for a moment, cursing himself for that last thought. It was bad enough he felt comfortable around Sean. Letting that comfort turn into anything more could ruin everything.

Sean's voice interrupted his thoughts. "You know, we're going to have to talk about what happened back there eventually."

"Do we have to?"

Sean paused. "I mean, technically no... but we should."

"There isn't much to say about it."

"I just don't want things to be awkward now."

Tirin raised an eyebrow. "Do you feel awkward about it?"

"Not really. I feel like I should, but somehow I don't."

Tirin let a small smile play on his lips. It was just like Sean to overthink everything. "So don't question it. Just let it be like that. There's no need to overcomplicate things."

"I know you're right. I guess that's just the person I am sometimes."

"I know. You love overthinking everything."

"I don't love it, I just do."

"I'm just pulling your leg." He nudged his shoulder.

Sean smiled. "I'm still not used to that from you."

"Teasing? Well, get used to it." He shrugged.

"You've always teased me, it's just never been in a good way I guess." Sean put a hand behind his neck.

Tirin rolled his eyes. "What did I say about getting yourself out of that head of yours? Just enjoy the moment."

"You know, it's funny that you can read me so well when I'm the one with the emotional abilities."

"You make it easy. I've come to know that you're a very expressive person."

Sean smiled before stopping in a decent cleared spot. "Does this spot look good?"

Tirin nodded and took his backpack off. He watched as Sean took out the pieces of the tent they had been using for the past few days. He should have been helping, and he knew that, but instead he just found himself watching. Sean was decently meticulous about the placement of the nails in the ground. He hammered them into the damp grass between the small loops of the tent sheet. After a moment he stopped and looked up.

"You're not going to criticize me?"

"What?" Tirin tensed.

"You always tell me I'm doing something wrong and then put up the tent yourself."

Tirin chuckled. "Well I don't feel like it this time, but you are placing the nails at a bad angle."

Sean rolled his eyes playfully. "Shut up."

"You asked." He shrugged, walking over to help him set up. After it was all set up he offered Sean his sleeping bag, remembering how he'd sacrificed his own the night before in the storm.

"Who are you and what have you done with the guy that hated me?"

"Just take it before I change my mind." He shoved the sleeping bag against his chest.Sean unfolded it and went into the tent. Tirin took a moment outside of the tent. He took a few deep breaths. He told himself over and over again that the lighthearted feeling was a good one. That it would be worth it to keep Sean smiling. That it was ok to want things that he wasn't used to wanting. Still, he didn't want to mess things up.

He made his way into the tent. He found himself hyper aware of how close they were. The image of holding him close the night before, frozen in his mind. He forced himself to relax, laying down on his back and breathing deeply. Unlike the previous nights, Sean hadn't chosen to lay down as far away as possible. He seemed comfortable near the middle of the tent. Tirin wasn't all the way against the tent wall either. It just felt natural that way. He turned his head, looking at Sean who was staring up at the tent's midpoint.

"Theoretically if I unzip the sleeping bag and spread the two ends out, it can be used like a blanket and cover both of us." Sean said suddenly.

"You do realize that It will still be small right?"

"And? Something is better than nothing." Sean began unzipping the sleeping bag.

Tirin tensed. He couldn't bring himself to believe that Sean understood how close they'd have to be to share the sleeping bag that way. Still, he wasn't going to say anything. He'd take the opportunity, then when Sean realized and pulled away, he'd just deal with it. He found that plan to be a good one. Sean spread out the sleeping bag over himself, turning it horizontally. Tirin scooted closer so that the edge of the blanket covered half of his body.

Sean turned to face him. "You're going to sleep like that?"

He met eyes with him for a moment, reading his expression. He realized Sean *did* understand what he was implying. He moved closer. Eventually, in order to get any decent coverage, he had to press himself against him lightly. Of course it didn't help that they were facing each other. In the dark of the tent he could make out parts of Sean's face more clearly now.

Sean's voice came out a bit shaky. "There, see? Now we can share it." He shifted, moving against Tirin. He tensed, unsure of his want to respond. He felt the heat of Sean's body. It was starting to get to him.

Sean must've noticed his reaction because he hesitated. "You don't need to be so tense. I'm not going to bite."

Tirin observed his face. He blinked, thinking he was seeing things until he was sure he was seeing it. The light shade of pink painted across Sean's face. He felt an odd warmth spread across his chest. He'd been physically close to people before, and yet he couldn't figure out why this time felt so different. Granted it was mostly women before, but it wasn't that big of a difference. He let himself relax against him.

"Better?" Sean looked up at him. Tirin nodded and gave a content sigh. "Good."

For a moment, he held his gaze. The silence pierced the air. He felt the need to do something. To pull him close. To do anything to fill the daunting space. Sean looked down for a moment. "Last night when you... can we...?"

Relief flooded through him as he wrapped his arms slowly around him. Sean let out a breath he'd been holding and Tirin felt his arms snake around him in return.

Sean continued looking up at him. "Does this... mean anything?"

Tirin hummed out a small laugh. "Does it have to?"

"I don't know." He watched as Sean confusion grew on his face, his cheeks still coated in a faint pink.

Tirin felt his hold tighten around him. He let go of his lighthearted tone. "Do you want it to mean something?"

Sean looked away. "Would it mess things up if I did?"

Tirin shrugged. "Maybe." In that moment, he decided that if he was going to be this close to him anyway, he might as well make it worth it. He put a hand under his chin and gently tilted it so he could pull his eyes back to his own. "Or, maybe not."

When Sean leaned in closer, he felt his breath grow shorter. In a single moment, Sean's eyes were half lidded, his hand was in his hair, and his lips were pressed against his own. The only thought he could focus on then, was how much more he wanted from him. How much more he *needed* from him. How much more he'd get even if it killed him.

Chapter 11
Sean

Tirin kissed him. *Tirin kissed him*, and he liked it. *It's just a kiss.* He told himself, over and over again as he got ready in the morning. He woke before Tirin, leaving the tent to clear his mind. He'd been pacing outside the tent opening for a good ten minutes before clutching his pendant and giving up on trying to wrap his head around what it all meant. He took a few deep breaths. Of course he was overthinking things. Tirin had been right. He was *always* overthinking things.

Maybe it didn't have to mean anything. They weren't teenagers. There was no reason to act like things were complicated. He concluded he'd try not to mention it when Tirin woke. If it meant nothing, then it did. If it meant something then it did. That was that. He had more important things to think about than a kiss that would probably only happen once.

He begged his own mind to focus on anything else but the kiss. It was then that he found himself thinking about how they'd get ahold of the Necrotanian object. He was starting to realize that every time they tried to make a plan it went wrong in all kinds of ways. They needed a back up plan this time. If Viera didn't challenge Tirin, or even worse, if Tirin didn't win, they'd be back at square one.

There was one other option. An option Tirin practically begged him not to consider. If the moment came when he'd have no other choice, he knew he'd give himself up. If he had to be killed, at least he could spare Tirin. At that realization, another dawned on him. He cared about Tirin. It wasn't just a normal care between partners. It was the kind of care that made him sure he'd rather sacrifice himself then let Tirin suffer with him if he could prevent it somehow.

It was a similar care to the one he'd felt for Antic back when they were close, yet it was still somehow different.

Even if he chose to completely ignore the physical attraction. The vague want to be close to him. The warmth of his arms around him, or even this kiss itself, it was all more than he'd felt for someone in a long time. Somehow that realization made everything worse in his mind instead of better.

The last thing they needed right now was something that could make everything more complicated. He decided it might be better to crawl up and die in a small hole in the ground, and even dug up and killed all over again, than face the absolute embarrassment of admitting his feelings to him. Especially when he was so sure it would go nowhere. If he had learned anything about Tirin over the last week together, it was how absolutely emotionally unavailable he was as a person. Sure, he had seen parts of his past, not by choice, but by a complete invasion of privacy. It made sense why he was so closed off, and it was childish to believe he would be the one to change that. So he cared about him. That didn't mean he had to act on it anytime soon, even if it nagged at him like a constant ache in the back of his mind.

Tirin came out of the tent. Sean stopped his pacing and looked at him, waiting for him to say something. When he didn't say a word he started for him, wanting anything but the awkward silence.

"Sleep ok?" He cringed internally at how awkward that sounded. Of course he had to say it like that.

"Could've been better." He shrugged nonchalantly, like he hadn't just half insulted Sean's ability to help him sleep. Not that it mattered to him, or at least he didn't want it to.

"That's... unfortunate." Sean said, trying not to sound disappointed.

Tirin smirked at his reaction. "I'm just teasing you know. I slept fine."

Sean managed a small smile. "Asshole."

Tirin chuckled, and somehow all of the tension in Sean's body left in an instant. Tirin began packing up, and Sean started breaking down the tent. About half way through, he stopped and looked up at Tirin expectedly.

Tirin huffed out a laugh. "You're doing it wrong."

Sean smiled. "Thank you. It's too weird if you don't say something."

Tirin rolled his eyes playfully, a smirk on his face. "Seriously though, you need to fold the poles before you wrap up the cover."

"You do it then." Sean crossed his arms.

"Fine." Tirin walked over and took the remainder of the tent from him. Sean froze up a bit as his hands brushed his own. He cursed himself. The touch wouldn't normally mean anything, but after the kiss... *the kiss*. Sean's mind spun as he watched him put away the tent.

As Tirin finished, he met his gaze. "What?"

Only then did Sean realize he'd been staring at him. "Nothing."

Tirin laughed. "Bullshit. I can see something on your face. What is it?"

Sean hesitated. He couldn't explain. Then he'd have to face rejection and possibly never ending teasing about it.

Tirin tilted his head. "Alright then. When you're ready, we'll talk."

Sean breathed a sigh of relief. It would've been a great opportunity to forget about the problem that was his feelings, except now all he could think about was how much he loved Tirin's patience and understanding. For a moment they lingered like that, some kind of comfortable silence between them. If comfortable meant hearing his heart in his chest beat louder with every passing second then that's what Sean concluded it to be. Tirin swung his backpack over his shoulder and motioned for Sean to follow him. He'd been so wrapped up in whatever this new fixation was that he'd forgotten the daunting depth of what they had to try and accomplish now just to keep his life at least a little longer.

In all honesty, who was to say that Antic would leave him alone even if the Sepratain object was unbound to him? He'd be killed for something even worse, the merging of the objects. The total sweep of the entire continate's ground under its feet and turning it over the population in one single moment. Everything they knew would change, the border, the culture, the ruling system, even the trials. All of that just so he could remain alive. Just so he could keep living, constantly reminded of the biggest mistake he'd ever made in his life. The more he thought about it, the more he felt like he didn't deserve it. He was about to sacrifice the sanity of an entire continent just to keep his insignificant failure of a life.

"What's that look?" Tirin's voice shattered his thoughts into pieces.

Sean walked beside him, almost dragging his feet. "What look?"

"The one where you act like a lost puppy."

Sean scoffed. "Is that seriously the only comparison you could think of?"

"I'm serious. You look like you're contemplating the meaning of life over there."

Not exactly the meaning of life, but the worth of his own life. Of course he refused to say it that way. All he managed was a weak smile and a "You know me."

"Fortunately." Sean had to backtrack in his mind for a second as he heard Tirin say the word. He was so used to the opposite coming from him that he felt like it wasn't even real, like he hadn't just heard him say that it wasn't just an ok thing that he knew him that way, but that it was a good thing. It was *fortunate* that he knew him that way. Then he was left to contemplate how he was in complete turmoil a moment ago and suddenly ok again all with a single word. He felt if he had to continue the rest of the day like this, he'd be exhausted within the hour from the absolute rollercoaster of his current emotional state.

Again Tirin ripped him out of his mind so fast it almost made his thoughts dizzy. "I don't know if I can beat her, even if she challenges me."

"I don't think we have any other option, unless..." Sean wanted to suddenly curl into himself, as if he could just hide from the world and never come back out.

"I already said that's not an option." Tirin's voice was firm. It was clear he didn't want to leave any room for arguing but Sean couldn't bring himself to care.

"And why do you get to say that?"

"What?" Tirin stopped walking, stunned.

"Why do you get to decide what I do with my life?"

"Sean, you can't be serious." Tirin grabbed his arm, forcing him to stop in front of him. He didn't say a word. Tirin frowned. "I'm not letting you do that. I don't care if I have to hold you back myself."

"We both know you can't do that." Sean pulled his arm out of his hand. He'd been practicing the object's power. With how close he'd come to beating him at the trials, he could take him. Especially with the power of the entire Sepratain object. He wouldn't stand a chance anymore. Just like that, his world shifted. He was actively choosing to play along. He could turn his back on him and give himself up at any moment.

"Don't make me prove I can." Tirin warned. His eyes narrowed on him.

"Why do you insist on suffering for me?" Sean felt the burning from the object through his wrist, clouding the edges of his vision. He didn't need a mirror to know that his eyes were dimly glowing white.

"I'm not suffering." Tirin stepped closer to him.

"Your life could be normal. What the hell do you have going for you if you try to protect me from Antic?" Tirin didn't back away, despite the way Sean's voice grew louder.

"You."

Sean froze, the dim glow in his eyes creeping out of his vision. "You don't mean that."

"I don't know how else to say it. I'm not suffering now. I was before but now, I'd rather fight the entire Sepratain forces and turn the continent on its head than let you walk out of my life just as quickly as you came into it." Tirin placed a gentle hand on his shoulder. "Read me."

"What?" Sean flinched.

"Let me show you that I'm not suffering." In an instant, Tirin grabbed his hand and pulled it to his shoulder. Sean focused on his energy. The aura around him wasn't at all like the usual smokey black cloud he carried. He was so wrapped up in his own mind that he hadn't even noticed the change. It was some kind of distant gray cloud, heavy and constant. The air around him was cold, but it was the kind of consistent prick underneath your arms that sent goosebumps through your body and made you want to seek the warmth of the nearest person. The kind of cold that Sean didn't mind. There wasn't an ounce of the usual burning anger he'd come to expect from him.

Sean forced himself to speak. "This isn't just because—" He couldn't bring himself to ask it.

Tirin shook his head. The one thing he was sure of about Tirin was his blunt honesty. The way his hand pulled him into an embrace made his mind blank, a low fog settling over it. Suddenly Sean was pulled out of the clouds in his mind back to the reality he hadn't wanted to face. A reality where Tirin actually cared about him. A reality where the kiss had meant something. A reality where he'd have to tilt the continent on its head just to keep himself alive even when he didn't deserve it. He felt Tirin's arms around him tighten, like he was afraid if he let go, Sean would disappear.

Chapter 12

Tirin

"I'm not letting you give yourself up."

He felt Sean surrender to the embrace. "Why?"

"Because you didn't give up on me. I'm not giving up on you, even if you've already given up on yourself." After everything he'd seen, Sean's persistence, his positive outlook, his self sacrifice, Tirin could only find it within himself to tell him the absolute truth. He deserved it. He deserved every ounce of the world Tirin could manage to give him. He'd die before he let him die by Antic's hand. The world didn't know it yet, but it was lucky to have Sean in it.

Finally, Sean melted into the embrace. "How did we get here?"

Tirin felt himself smile. "You have a way of messing up people's plans."

"You diverted first." Sean laughed and Tirin swore he felt a single tear splash his shoulder.

"I guess you won't be the only one with a major object soon."

"Never thought you'd join the fuck up club."

Tirin shifted his hold on him. "You didn't give me much of a choice."

***

For once, walking next to Sean wasn't the worst thing in the world. He wasn't sure how but it felt like the opposite now. There was so much he'd never noticed about him, so much he wanted to know. Even though he'd kissed him, it was like they'd taken a step backwards and somehow forwards at the same time. Now he could get to know him, the real him. The guy who didn't like tomatoes and had a strange obsession with collecting rocks. The guy who'd messed up the mission so incredibly badly and somehow found his way into the walls Tirin worked a lifetime to build. The guy whose lips felt softer than any girl Tirin had ever been with. *It's just a kiss.* Tirin had to remind himself that they hadn't agreed on it meaning anything. Even though it meant the world to him.

Sean suddenly stopped his adorable rambling. Tirin hadn't even noticed the figures approaching them until now. He put a hand in front of Sean, stopping him in his tracks. It took a few long seconds for the figures to come into view enough to recognize them. Sean visibly relaxed but Tirin stayed on edge.

"Gem." Sean spoke first.

He tried to walk forward but Tirin held his arms firmly in front of him. "I don't think we have time to get captured again. She chose her side."

"We can tell her about the Neutral object."

"They aren't going to listen. Think about it. Do you really think the VAA would appreciate turning the continent for a new one like we're planning to do? The normal continent is already afraid of us."Tirin saw his contemplation. He paused as more figures came into view behind Gem. His expression grimmed.

Once she got close enough, she spoke. "Hand over the object Sean."

"We don't have it." Tirin said sharply.

"I'm having a hard time believing that after you broke out of headquarters to chase it down."

"Gem, you have to listen to us." Sean pleaded.

"I'm trying to protect you Sean. All you had to do was follow the plan, but you can't ever seem to do that right."

Tirin felt Sean tense under his arm. "You were going to the wrong place. I had to do something."

Gem looked at him longingly. "Don't make me do this."

"You can't be serious. You'd pick the VAA over your own brother?"

"I get to be something with them. More than I could ever be with you around." Tirin felt a burning pain grow in his chest. The other figures, VAA officers. They started encircling the pair cautiously. He felt the cold sting of his object's power spread from the tip of his ear down his neck. He could see the way Sean's eyes dimly lit. They shifted, back to back.

"I'd be careful if I were you. It doesn't have to be this hard."

Tirin scoffed. "You're right, it doesn't."

Gem frowned. "I'm sorry. I didn't want to do this." The way she repeatedly said it made Tirin think she wanted to be sure the pair knew she didn't have bad intentions. Of course it didn't matter what intentions she had, her brother could die if she caught them. For Tirin, that was enough to get his blood boiling.

Without another word, Gem gave a hand signal and the VAA officers began closing in slowly. Tirin felt the cold spark of his object spread from his neck to his hands in an instant. He focused on the sensation, letting it build for a moment before bringing his hands up slowly into the air in front of him. A few dark Necrotanian portals around the size of a basketball opened on the ground. Skeletal hands sprung from them, grabbing a few of the agents by their ankles. It wasn't much but it was enough to slow some of them down.

Sean channeled a small bust of energy through his hands, the white glow piercing the air as it burned and knocked a couple of agents down. One of the officers pulled out a strange looking type of gun from the holder at his side. In the second he had to react, Tirin pushed Sean and himself out of the way. A loud pulverising sound cracked as the gun shot a bright blue blast fading off into the trees around them. Tirin glared back at the officer. He focused on the tingling sensation at his fingertips, calling a cold, dark blast at them. The agent was swift enough to move out the way. He knew he'd have to work to disarm them somehow. He charged at the agent, preparing to dodge the next blast they tried to fire.He dove out of the way of the blue circles and tackled the officer, knocking the blaster out of his hands.

No more than ten seconds later, he heard all kinds of screams coming from Sean's direction. He quickly knocked the officer across the head, causing them to lose consciousness. He then got up and stared back at Sean. His eyes went wide as he saw Sean, holding three officers by the throat with Sepratain vines. Even using all that power, he somehow still had enough left to summon a larger portal in the air. Tirin knew exactly what kind of creature he was calling. He shook himself out of it and ran towards the remaining officers, taking them out one by one. In his moment of hesitance, he was unable to stop Gem from making it to Sean's side.

Tirin watched as Sean forced the vines holding the officers to the ground as hard as he physically could. He yelled at her through the sounds of the bodies crashing down on the Earth. "If I had the Neutral object, I wouldn't still be bound to the Sepratain one."

"That doesn't mean you're allowed to escape again." Gem was different, blinded by something. He could see it in her eyes. Tirin made his way closer, but in the end he knew that the fight had to be between them.

"I don't have time to be kept in a makeshift prison. Antic is going to find me eventually and when that happens, he'll kill me. You can be as angry as you want, but I know you don't want me dead." Sean said, pulling vines up out of the ground around Gem.

Gem avoided the vines, pulling out a blaster similar to the one the other agent had used. "I'll protect you like I always have. You won't die and I'll clean up the mess you made as usual."

"You're willing to take that risk, even if it means I could die? You can't honestly tell me you believe the VAA has a chance against the Sepratain forces."

Gem shot a blast at Sean. He was quick enough to avoid it, his eyes glowing brighter as the portal above continued to summon some kind of Sepratain creature. Gem charged towards him. "I do, Sean. I have a chance at protecting you. If this is how I have to do it then so be it."

Sean shot a minor blast at her, not intended to do much damage. She ducked out of the way. "You don't have to prove yourself to me like everyone else. I know how strong you are. You always have been."

His final attempt to get through to her, didn't seem to be enough. Tirin, finally by Sean's side, summoned a handful of skeletons to keep her busy. The portal above finally finished. A large winged creature flew out of it and down by Sean's side. Tirin hadn't ever seen that kind of creature up close.He decided now wasn't the time to be astounded. He hopped up on the creature and helped Sean up. The creature started to fly without a second thought. Tirin held onto Sean, knowing it must've taken a lot out of him to summon such a creature. Sean watched Gem disappear from view. The moment she was out of sight he practically collapsed against Tirin.

Tirin caught him, letting his concern show in his eyes. Sean breathed heavily. The creature wouldn't last long, the most they could do is cut a few long hours of travel off their trip. Tirin put a hand on Sean's face.

Sean looked up at him, his eyes heavy. "I'm ok."

"And you did great." Tirin said.

Sean smiled at him. That smile that made every second of the fight worth it. "You too."

"Get some rest." Tirin said, running his hand slowly along his cheek. Sean didn't say another word, exhaustion taking over his body. He closed his eyes. Tirin watched him rest, the flying creature slowly descending after a good amount of distance. He observed the creature, the feathered wings, the large talons, it was incredible. He wondered where Sean had learned to do that. It didn't matter now, he thought. All that mattered to him was Sean. *Safe*.

Chapter 13
Sean

The first thing Sean felt when he woke, was the warmth of Tirin's embrace. He looked up at him. Tirin's gaze fell on him like he was precious.

"As much as I'd like to let you keep resting, we have to keep moving."

Sean sat up, his back still against him. It was then that he realized they were on the ground. "The creature?"

"It dematerialised 5 minutes after you fell asleep." Tirin made no attempt to pull away from him, his arms still around his chest.

"Where are we now?"

"About a mile out from Necrotan."

Sean shifted, looking at the ground. "What about Gem?"

Tirin ran a comforting hand through his hair. "The Skeletons wouldn't have held her back for long. She'll be fine."

Sean nodded, allowing the comfort of Tirin's touch to wash over him. After a moment passed, Tirin began to move. Reluctantly, Sean stood beside him. He still felt dazed, like the fog of a hangover rested over his thoughts.

"Let's hope they were the only ones to find us for now. I don't think you have the strength to do that again, at least not for a while." Sean felt Tirin's hand grab his as he spoke. An odd warmth spread through his chest. Tirin walked at a slower pace than usual. Sean grew a small smile as he processed the way Tirin seemed to care for him. He found himself thinking about their relationship as they walked. They'd come a long way. He thought about the way they fought, the things they'd said to each other. Then the memories in the temple. The way they'd held each other that night. *The kiss.*

The kiss that didn't seem to mean anything and yet it had changed everything about the way he saw their interactions now. He couldn't help but feel like he was thinking about this as if he was still in high school. It wasn't his first kiss. It wasn't even his first kiss with a guy. He'd come out as gay a long time ago. Yet here he was overthinking things, just like always. He decided then, that he would stop. That he'd just let it be for once. Maybe this was something that was better left the way it was in his mind. A beautiful memory that meant whatever he wanted it to mean. A thing between them that could turn into anything they made it. He smiled to himself at that thought.

***

It wasn't long before they'd reached the edge of Necrotan. Sean felt a sense of peace being back across the border. The familiar streets and territory made the whole situation feel just a little safer. On this side of the border they most likely wouldn't be attacked by the Sepratain forces out in the open. That kind of thing could be read as a political statement, especially with the border laws Antic had been talking about setting during his coronation speech. Sean was sure he wasn't crazy enough to risk that kind of tension within the country.

The only thing they'd really have to worry about now was Sean's new tendency to be read as Sepratain alliance thanks to the object. It wouldn't be a huge problem. Necrotanians were far less judgey than Sepratain people, or at least that's how Sean felt about it. But his presence would probably make a few people uncomfortable. Of course him being a wanted criminal across the border was sure to be known by now. They'd have to worry about being seen by the Necrotanian guard every now and again, but they most likely wouldn't be intentionally pursued by them. After all it wasn't Necrotan's problem, and the new heir wouldn't give two shits about it, unless it benefited her directly in some way.

They'd met before at the trials, Sean and Viera the current heir to the Necrotanian object. Of course there was no way she'd remember Sean. If she'd gotten the chance to fight him, she'd beat him in a heartbeat. They met by chance. She'd dropped her bag in the waiting room and Sean helped her pick it up. They exchanged a few words. That was the end of it. Looking back Sean was hit with the realization that she might've done it on purpose. With the type of person she was, she could've just been scouting out who might be the type of person to do that sort of thing.

She'd definitely remember Tirin. They fought in one of the semi final rounds. She beat him, not easily, but it wasn't that close of a match. She was a lot stronger than anyone had realized. The kind of person that looks easy to fight, but wins because you underestimate them. But there was one thing about her that was instantly noticeable. She was full of herself. Everything she said in her coronation speech had some kind of self promotion. The kind of cocky attitude that came off as way too much. If you could get her talking about herself, she might not stop for the next hour. It also meant that she had absolutely no care for insults. You could say whatever you wanted to try and get in her head, but she'd never take it to heart. Sean had felt her aura once before. Green, bright, and so unbelievably hard to influence.

Most people had some kind of cloudy aura around them that Sean had learned to read and influence, but some people had a kind of fog that was hard to see through. It was easy to read, but if you tried to influence it, the fog would nearly strangle you. It was heavy and thick. The kind of beach side salty air that never left your lungs. Viera was one of those people. If Tirin was going to fight her, Sean wouldn't be much help. His mind lingered on that thought. Tirin never really planned things out. He wasn't that kind of person. He found himself wondering how it would play out in the end. If Viera won, they'd risk everything for nothing.

"I wish we could just run." Sean spoke his mind as they walked along the empty street. They'd taken the backroad to the castle so they could stay decently hidden.

Tirin looked at him for a moment, confused at the sudden statement. "What?"

"To the normal continent or to the edge of the world. To a place where no one could find us or bother us."

Tirin gave his hand a playful squeeze. "Are you saying you'd want to run away with me?"

Now that was a vision Sean's mind wanted to hold onto. The image of a small place, hidden from the world, no one could ever find. A place where he could be himself and no one could judge him. A place where he could live out his days in peace. Of course it was a dream that could never be reality.

"I'm saying I'd run away if I could. You coming with me would just be an added bonus."

Tirin smirked. "You're crazy if you think I'd let you do that alone. You'd get found in a couple days without me to cover your clumsy tracks."

Sean smiled. "I'm serious, you know."

"Maybe we could've before all of this. Before the VAA roped us into this mess. But then, it wouldn't be an 'us' idea. We would probably still hate each other."

"But imagine if we didn't. How good that would be."

"You know, before if you would've asked me, I'd probably say you were an idiot for even imagining it, but now… now it's a dream. Now it's something I'm imagining with you."

Tirin smiled, a real smile. One that Sean had been waiting to see. He felt his chest warm again and in that moment he wished he could stay there. Stay imagining that beautiful future. Stay in that peaceful place in his mind. Stay with the side of Tirin that always seemed to know exactly what to say. The version of him whose emotional aura was a soft gray cloud that collided with his own swirl of an autumn breeze.

But as they turned towards a main street and the ground shook beneath them, he knew instantly that it wasn't meant to be.

Chapter 14
Tirin

I f there was any kind of power in the universe, it was cruel to break that beautiful moment. Tirin never imagined he'd ever want that kind of thing to keep going, but as the ground began to shake beneath them, he wished it could never end. He gripped Sean's hand a little tighter, prepared to protect him. The prick of his neck hairs standing up told him something was coming. He felt the cold gentle stab of his power spark at the tip of his ear. He glanced down the end of the main street. Then in the distance, it was clear.

People around them started to run out of the street in a panic. Some just stopped and stared at the absolute army of Sepratain forces marching directly through the middle of the main road. In the center of them, Antic held a flag

Tirin had never seen before, almost like a symbol of whatever crazy separation he was planning. He knew Antic was an extreme kind of guy, but he never imagined that kind of political statement coming from him. He tugged Sean along the side of a building, trying to disappear behind it.

"We need to hide."

"He can't be serious." Tirin hadn't even taken the time to notice the way Sean seemed to be hyperventilating. He was breathing frantically. His hands were shaking. His eyes darted along the surrounding area like he couldn't focus on a single thing, looking for some kind of escape.

"Sean?"

"It's too soon. He's going to start a movement like this." He leaned against the wall of the building like he could collapse without its support.

"Sean." Tirin lowered his voice, trying to get his attention. He squeezed his hand gently.

"How are we going to-"

"Sean." Tirin cut him off, pulling him by the shoulders into a tight embrace. "It's going to be ok." Sean tensed for a moment, freezing in place before slowly returning the embrace with a hesitance that made Tirin's chest ache. "Breath. Just breathe." He slowed his own breathing, purposely exaggerating to get him to follow his pace. "Just copy me."

Sean gave in, instantly tightening his hold around him. He held him like he was some kind of life line. They stood like that for a few long moments. With each slow breath Tirin could feel Sean relax his body just a little bit more. He spoke, his voice low in an attempt to ground him. "Stay with me. Here. It's just you and me."

Sean nodded slowly into his shoulder. He mumbled. "What are we going to do?"

"Let me worry about that. You just focus on breathing right now." Tirin let him hold on for a little longer before slowly pulling away. He kept his fingers entwined with his, slowly beginning to pull him along the sides of buildings to keep out of sight.

"They're heading where we are. I don't know what he's planning but it involves going to the castle."

"How did they know we were going there?"

"I'm not sure if they do. There's clearly something we're missing going on here."

Sean hesitated before speaking. "Do you think Gem-"

"No. She might be trying to capture us, but there is no way she wants you dead. She wouldn't give you to Antic like that, at least not without some kind of motive."

Sean let out a breath he must've been holding in, relieved. "Right."

"We need to get to the castle before they do."

"Are you sure that's the right move?"

"Viera won't be fond of us being there in a situation like this, but at the very least she's one to try and protect her own people."

Sean looked at him like he was crazy. "You say that like she's been ruling Necrotan for longer than a few days."

"Thinking about the type of person she is, I know she'll be decent at this, and she'll have bigger problems to worry about than the fourth heir."

"The fourth heir who's about to walk in with a wanted criminal and who she'll think brought Antic here in the first place. What if she takes his side and just hands us over? Plus I don't think she'll be too thrilled to hear that we're planning to challenge her if she realizes that Antic is about to capture us."

"Ok so it's a risk and it's not the best plan. Got any better ideas? If we don't get there first, Antic might convince her never to let us challenge her. Then we'd have no chance at getting the object in the first place." Tirin didn't wait for Sean to agree. He pulled him along by their connected hands as he started down the path he knew would get them to the castle faster.

"Wait-" Sean pulled him back for a moment. "If this is the last time we're going to have peace like this..." He put his hand on tirin's shoulder, a familiar sensation. "Just let me show you something first."

"We don't have time to wait any longer. Every second here is another second Antic get's closer to the castle."

"Just... please..." Sean pendant started to glow beneath his shirt. Tirin knew what he was doing. He was trying to influence his emotions, but he didn't understand what for. Normally when he did that, it was only to calm him down when he was angry to give his mind peace in moments of adrenaline, but this wasn't one of those times. He sighed, figuring Sean would press until he let him do it. It would be faster just to give in.

"Alright." He stood still, allowing Sean to influence him. It took less than five seconds for Tirin to feel something, the soothing energy pulsing through his shoulder from the point of contact, but something was different. There was something warmer to this energy. Something he didn't recognize. He closed his eyes, focusing on the way the warm feeling spread through his chest like wildfire. It wasn't a bad feeling. It wasn't exactly a feeling he was used to either. It was softer somehow.

Tirin opened his eyes to see Sean's staring back at him, something different about them. "Why is it different?" His voice came out a little strained. It was then that he felt the warmth spread to his face. A few more moments and his face felt like it was sparking with a bit of heat.

"I don't know..." Sean said.

"What do you mean you don't know?" Sean looked away like he had some idea, Tirin guessed he knew more than he was letting on.

"I just wanted to show you..."

Tirin finally understood. Sean's power was often connected to his own emotions. He completed his sentence for him. "...how you're feeling."

Sean nodded. His grey eyes locked with Tirin's own for a moment. He thought he'd never find the strength to pull away, but the rumble of the ground every now and again as Antic's army of soldiers stepped ever closer made his mind snap out of it. He held Sean's hand, gently this time. "I understand."

Sean gave him a small smile. That kind that made his already warm chest intensify like it had burst into flames. He watched as Sean took a deep breath and steadied himself. "I'm ready now."

***

As they neared the castle, having taken the back roads to remain hidden and hopefully make it there faster, Tirin found himself thinking for once. Not just any kind of thinking either. The kind of thinking Sean did all the time. The dangerous kind of thinking. Overthinking. It wasn't like him to get in his head that way, but as they got closer and closer to the castle's doors, he felt a pit in his stomach that wouldn't seem to close. A hole that grew larger with every small squeeze of Sean's hand.

He was never afraid before, not even for a second but now there was something to be afraid of. Someone to care about. Someone to protect. Someone he'd never want to lose. He'd just grown attached to him, and that very person who was holding his hand, had the entire world after him, threatening to take him away the instant he let go long enough. He wouldn't dare let go now.

"That's far enough." As they came to the castle and approached the doors a guard's voice snapped him out of his thoughts.

Tirin flashed him a look of annoyance thinking the guard was a new hire. He flashed his earring and held out his arm to be read for the magical alliance. "I'm Tirin Stirn. Fourth heir."

"I know that, but HE won't be allowed any further."

"He's coming in with me. We need to speak to Viera and trust me she'll want to hear what he has to say."

The guard tensed. "But he's a wanted criminal."

"Conflicts across the border are not our problem. Now let us in." He demanded.

"*I'm afraid he can't do that.*" Antic's voice hit him like a ton of bricks as the door to the castle swung open. They were too late. Tirin instinctively put his arm in front of Sean, standing his ground. He felt the way Sean trembled under his touch, and it made the pit in his stomach clench and grow all at once.

"Well look who's playing guard dog now. I thought you wanted nothing to do with him." Antic practically taunted him.

"You're not taking him."

"You think your words are going to stop me? That's pathetic." Antic made a motion with his arms. A swarm of soldiers came to enclose a circle around them. Tirin felt the spark of cold energy prick at his ear from the object. He felt the dim glow of his eyes as the power started to travel through his veins.

"I wouldn't do that if I were you. I've got you surrounded, and you'll only make things worse for yourself."

His attention shifted as Sean placed a hand on his shoulder with an intense pulse of calming energy. He looked back at him, unsure what he was thinking, but the look in his eyes wasn't angry or even afraid. He sighed, pushing Tirin's arm out of the way.

"This is between us, Antic. You have no business making other people suffer for me."

"You're the one making them suffer. Of course it doesn't have to be that way. You could just come with me willingly, and maybe I'll think about letting your sister go." He stepped aside, revealing Gem behind him, on her knees, held there by Sepratain soldiers.

Tirin felt Sean tense before he spoke. "This isn't you. I know you, the guy I'd been friends with for years, is still in there. Please, come back to me and let all of this go." Sean took a careful step forward. Tirin raked his mind looking for a way out of the situation. He knew Sean's pleading wouldn't work. Whoever Antic was before, he wasn't that guy anymore. His eyes darted around him as he tried to come up with a plan.

"You don't know me Sean. I always put in the effort to show you who I was but you never really saw it. Your eyes were always... elsewhere."

"Then let me listen now. Show me who you are and I promise it won't be like before."

Antic clenched his fist by his sides. "Don't make promises you can't keep. I'm done giving you chances. If you're just going to keep hurting me then I'm going to hurt you. You'll know the pain you put me through, and it starts here." Antic drew out a thin blade from his side. He carefully positioned it underneath Gem's neck. "Come with me now, or you'll be the reason she dies with you."

Tirin watched the way Sean's eyes went from Gem to Antic, as if he was reading him, like he still couldn't believe Antic would threaten him that way. Tirin put a hand on his arm.

"Oh, and maybe I'll let your little boy toy live too." Tirin grimaced. He wasn't anyone's 'boy toy'.

He leaned in and spoke lowly. "Let me know when you're ready and I'll blast his face in." Sean always had a plan. He knew this would only go so long before he started to enact the fight that would get them out of here. But then he saw Sean's expression.

"Tirin..." The tone in his voice made his blood run cold. "Haven't I caused you enough trouble?"

Tirin lowered his voice, a sense of frustration building. "We talked about this. I'm not letting him take you."

"You deserve peace. The whole continent does, and we both know that'll only happen if I do this..."

Tirin squeezed his arm tightly. "There has to be another way out of this. You'll have to kill me before I let them take you."

"You won't have to." Sean pressed a swift kiss to his cheek. The feeling lingered, but he pulled away before Tirin even had time to process the action. "Keep Gem out of trouble for me." The hand on Tirin's shoulder pulsed again, a feeling that made Tirin's whole body freeze up for a few split seconds, long enough for Sean to wiggle out of his grip on his arm.

"Don't do this!" he shouted, the crackle at his ears sparked as he called skeletal hands from the ground in an attempt to stop him. The encroaching guards grabbed him, pulling at his arms. He couldn't do anything but watch as Sean walked towards Antic.

"What a sweet reunion this had been. Don't worry my friend, I'll make our remaining time together something to remember." Antic wrapped an arm around Sean tauntingly. The gesture only made the fire in Tirin's chest spark out of control. He punched one of the guys holding him, the blow uncontrolled and sending the guard to the ground. He fought hard, not letting up with all of his strength. The only thing he could focus on was Antic's arm around Sean, pulling him down the path back towards the border. A long white vehicle waiting for them.

Tirin felt the strain of his throat as he shouted at him. "I'll fucking kill you!"

He watched as they got into the vehicle and drove away, the guards not letting up their attack until a few long minutes after they'd gone.

Gem stumbled to her feet, tears in her eyes. She walked over to Tirin. "I'm so sorr-"

He interrupted her, his fist meeting her face in a hard punch. His anger was too far gone now to even see clearly, the edges of his eyes blurred. "This is YOUR fault. If you had focused on protecting him instead of trying to capture us, he'd still be here."

Gem cursed, putting a hand on her face and practically growling back at him. "I was trying to protect him. If you two had just stayed at headquarters, things could've been better."

"Stayed at headquarters? You mean sit idly by while you lead the VAA to the wrong location to search for an object that doesn't even exist!"

Gem stepped back, stunned.

"Don't give me that bullshit look. Do you think he'd still have the object bound to him if we'd found it? We tried to tell you but you were so fixated on keeping your god dam position in the association that you got your own brother killed!"

"That's enough." She said, balling her fists at her sides.

Tirin grabbed her by the shirt. "You took the only good thing in my life away from me!" The words flew out before he could think about any sort of consequences.

"I said THAT'S ENOUGH!" She shouted back, shoving him hard and causing him to stumble. "Whatever this is, it's not going to bring him back here. Unless you want to just let Antic kill him, we need to think of a plan. Fast."

A tall young looking man approached them from the castle steps. His voice rang out like he had no care in the world. "We're going to get Sean Hallow back, don't you worry."

Tirin couldn't bring the harsh tone out of his voice in his fit of rage. "Who the hell are you?"

"Someone who can get you what you need." He ran a hand through his short blond hair and pointed at the castle doors. "I'm assuming you were here for a reason right? Viera and I have some history you could say."

"That doesn't answer my question."

He laughed. "Do I really need to spell it out for you? I'm the leader of *Sean's revolution*."

Chapter 15

Sean

He wasn't dead yet, but that fact became less and less appealing as the hours turned into days. At one point he almost wished death would come so the cycle could end. He had known all along that it wasn't Antic's intention to kill him immediately, but whatever sick game he expected him to play was far from this one. The drugs he'd been given were starting to kick in now. It didn't matter how used to the stench of the place he was by now, he was thankful at least that part would fade away. He felt his mind slip away from him, becoming a hazy mess. Even when he knew he was alone, all he could hear was Antic's cold voice echoing along the walls of the prison cell.

Don't worry my friend, I'll make our remaining time together something to remember. He could still see the way he grinned at him. The sinister look Sean felt he'd been missing all this time. His thoughts were interrupted by the sound of footsteps approaching the cell. Just when he thought he could escape it, there it was again, that taunting voice.

"Is there anything you want handsome?"

Sean didn't answer. He was tired of his mocking and he felt if he stopped giving him attention he might give him mercy and kill him already.

Antic hummed. "Don't be so salty, I'm only asking because you deserve a last request. I'm not that much of a monster."

"You are a *monster*." He said bitterly.

"Come now, is that any way to treat an old friend?" Antic opened the door to the cell and stepped inside, the bars creaking as he closed the gate behind him.

Sean shifted out of his curled up position, chains rattling at his wrist. "Whatever you're going to do, just get it over with already."

Antic walked over to him crouching down in front of him. "Aww but that's no fun. Don't you think there should be more to your last days of existence?"

He was close enough now that Sean could read his emotional aura. It was a heavy fog, masking just about everything but there was something he could see through it, even with the haze of the drugs, some underlying pain with every word he spoke. He carried it like a weight over his shoulders. It wasn't any kind of guilt or remorse at what he was doing to him, but a deeper pain, one rooted within the depth of himself.

"I do have a last request."

Antic raised an eyebrow curiously, smirking. "And what's that handsome?"

Sean placed a hesitant hand on his shoulder. "Let me take the pain away from you."

Antic hesitated like he might actually have considered it for a moment, but that moment was short lived. "The pain I feel serves a purpose. It's a reminder of what happens when I trust people and let my sight be blinded by foolish emotions. A consequence of the things I have to do to keep the new era of Sepratain moving forward."

"It's my last request. Just let me take away that pain. Let me undo what I've made you become." Some part of him had come up with a delusion that taking the pain away might undo everything. All his mistakes and the way he failed him as a friend all that time ago.

Antic hummed a small breathless laugh, gently grabbing Sean's chin and rubbing his thumb along his bottom lip as he tilted his head upward. "You haven't made me do anything. Sure you were a catalyst for my realization of what I needed to do and accomplish, but I've done everything I have on my own accord. That's the beauty of free will, handsome." His cold blue eyes had an intense stare that Sean wasn't used to. The way the blue contrasted his dark hair drew even more attention to them.

"If you're not going to take my request then what now? Are you planning to torture me until you're satisfied and then kill me?"

Antic drew his face closer., his breath warm against his skin. "You could say that." He let tnge silence linger in the air for a moment before speaking again. "But actually, I'm not going to kill you for now. I'd rather make sure that any time anyone ever gets close to you again, all you'll be able to see in them is me. My face. My anger. My pain. All the things you've done to fail me and others. You'll remember it everytime you look into someone's eyes. Everytime you brush another person's touch. You won't be able to escape me, even in the darkest corners of your mind."

***

The first time he heard him, his soul felt alive again. The last time he heard him, he wanted to die. He wanted so badly for it to be real. He told himself over and over again that it was normal to doubt that kind of thing after all he'd been through. The brain always has different ways of processing things. Sometimes he didn't mind seeing him. It gave him solace in moments of tragedy. Then Antic was there, and that solace was ripped away from him. Maybe it was a subconscious cry for help, something his mind did to try and ease the pain. Maybe it was the drugs, but he saw Tirin every time he turned around. And every time, just as he got close, Antic was there. Just like he said. In the darkest corners of his mind. Even when no one was there, he was. He ALWAYS was.

Chapter 16

Tirin

Tempest was annoying. Most people were to Tirin, but he was a whole other brand of *just shut up already*. He almost never stopped talking and none of what he said was useful information unless you asked him a direct question. It was all wrapped in some metaphor as if he loved to confuse people instead of giving them a direct answer. The other thing that didn't make sense about him, is how he somehow had higher priority around the castle then Tirin himself did as fourth heir to the Necrotanian object. He didn't even look Necrotanian but he had to be considering his magical alliance was read at the gates by the guards.

Tirin found himself trying to block out the nagging sound of his voice as they walked through the halls of the castle. It's a good thing Gem was listening to him because he almost missed the important information.

"You're kidding right?" She asked with an expression of disbelief.

"Why would I joke about something like that?" He placed his hands on his hips like he was offended she'd asked.

Gem raised an eyebrow. "I've just met you so it could be for a number of reasons."

"Why is it so hard to believe? Sean is revolutionary, of course there are people who are willing to stand for his cause."

That's when he got Tirin's attention. Sean and revolutionary shouldn't have been in the same sentence. Sure he cared about him now but that didn't make him any less of an idiot. He laughed. "What about Sean is revolutionary?"

"You don't just bind to the Sepratain object by accident. He started a movement. A protest. A revolution. A realization that the system needs to change."

Tirin and Gem met eyes. His own mirroring the question between them, *should we tell him?* She shook her head as if to say, *of course not.* He rolled his eyes. "None of that explains why you have a higher clearance than me here."

Tempest laughed, flaunting his wrist. "Listen, tall, dark and brooding. There are other ways to be influential in this world than placing well in the trials. It's called having connections. Ever heard of it?"

Tirin's chest burned. He was already pissed off enough while trying to deal with Antic taking Sean. He was NOT in the mood to handle an attitude like Tempest's. "Can you just give one goddamn direct answer?"

Tempest feigned offence, placing a hand over his chest. "Where's the fun in that? But fine, I suppose I can offer some easily understandable information for the troubled mind. Viera is my fiance."

Gem looked at him in shock. "So let me get this straight. You're the leader of a revolution against the heir system AND you're engaged to a woman who took the throne because of the heir system."

Tempest winked. "Give the girl a prize. She's put it together ladies and gentlemen."

Tirin decided that he needed a moment to himself to calm down or he'd punch this guy's face in. He tried to imagine Sean's hand on his shoulder and the calming feeling he'd get from it, but that made him think about the last time. The way the feeling was warmer, softer. The way he'd smiled at him. The way he'd given himself to Antic. Then his blood boiled again. Calming down that way wasn't going to work. If they were going to get Sean back, he needed to clear his head and focus. He desperately wished he could just turn around now, barge into the Sepratain palace and kill the damn bastard that took Sean away from him, but he knew that wouldn't get anywhere. Even if he could go in guns blazing, it wouldn't solve the problem of Sean being bound to the object. He had to challenge Viera first. It was the only way forward.

"So what's your plan, hot head?" Tempest nudged his shoulder.

He looked away not wanting to admit that he had no idea how he was going to beat her even if she accepted the challenge. He tried coming up with an excuse in his head but when that didn't sound quite right all he said was, "To challenge her."

"Well thanks captain obvious, but I mean how do you plan to beat her when she kicked your ass in the trials?" Tirin looked away for a split second and Tempest laughed. "Don't tell me you don't have a plan at all."

Gem glanced at him. Tirin didn't meet her eyes. Sean was the planner not him. He was supposed to know how to fix things or get out of situations. But he wasn't there, and Tirin seemed to be constantly reminded of that. He managed a sentence through gritted teeth. "Sean had a plan."

"Wait a second, aren't you the guy who got Sean disqualified from the trials? How'd you end up in his circle?"

"I didn't get him disqualified. He did it himself, I just knew how to push him to do it." He mentally kicked himself realizing that didn't sound any better at all if not worse.

Tempest seemed to be finding his anger amusing. "Don't worry I get it. He's the brains, you're the braun. Though I'm not so sure you're even good at that part considering you let him get captured."

Now he crossed a line. Tirin gripped the front collar of his shirt, stopping their walking and glaring at him. "I did not let him get captured. He gave himself up."

"Oh, looks like I struck a chord with that one huh?" He didn't seem startled in the slightest. He just smirked like it was his goal to get under his skin.

"I don't know what your deal is but you need to watch your mouth before I lose my patience."

Gem put a hand on Tirin's shoulder, her touch a bit rough, the way it had been when she'd stopped him and Sean from fighting when they were a team. "Tirin, don't. We need him."

"You should listen to the girl, hot head. Do you really want to waste time here while Sean gets closer to his death?" That stupid smirk wouldn't leave his face. Tirin squeezed his eyes shut for a moment before sighing and letting him go. Gem's hand felt lighter against his shoulder and for a moment he could almost convince himself it was Sean. He had to get him back. He felt like he was losing his mind.

"Well, if you don't have a plan, I do, but you might not like it."

***

Really? That was his plan? Tirin wanted to grab him by the neck and choke him to death as he heard his voice.

"Viera. My love. My darling angel. I'm so happy to-"

"No." Viera crossed her arms. "Whatever you're about to ask of me, the answer is no."

Tirin watched as Tempest pouted like a child, extending his bottom lip. "But darling, won't you at least hear me out this time?"

Viera seemed unamused. "The last time I heard you out, you destroyed my favorite painting."

"You know I didn't mean that. It was an accident my love."

"Well I don't have time for more of your *accidents*."

Tirin rolled his eyes before acknowledging her. "Long time no see."

She nodded, patting Tempest gently on the top of his head. "What's he roped you into? And before you answer, you should know that Antic told me everything."

"Whatever he's told you, I can assure you it's far from the truth."

"Really? So Sean hasn't stolen the Sepratain object? You haven't helped him escape several times and been his accomplice? You're not here to do the same to my object?"

Tirin winced, trying to find a better way to explain himself that didn't sound as criminal. He was never good at de-escalation. Sean always did the talking. "It's not *exactly* like that..."

Viera rolled her eyes. "I know what you're going to do, and I accept."

Tirin raised an eyebrow. "What?"

"You're here to challenge me for the object right?" She idly ran a hand through Tempest's hair. "I accept."

Gem huffed out a laugh behind him. "That was fast."

"We both know you aren't going to win anyways so we might as well make it a good time." She started, putting out a hand for the official handshake of the challenge. Tirin hesitated. Sure this was his plan but he'd expected it to be a lot harder to convince her. The worst part was that he had no plan at all and he felt like it was destined to go horribly wrong. He'd already failed at protecting Sean, he couldn't fail at this too. He *wouldn't*.

Chapter 17
Sean

He didn't know how long he'd been there. It could've been days. It could've been weeks. It all began to fade together in his mind. The hazy feeling of the drugs they'd given him to subdue his object abilities made it hard to focus on anything at all during that time. At some point he heard footsteps as usual coming from the entrance to the dungeon. He didn't bother looking at him.

"If you're going to kill me, just do it already." He said solemnly.

"I'm not here for that." Sean looked up to see a man with golden blond hair done slightly over his face.

Sean kept his eyes down, thinking it could be a guard out of uniform. "Then you're here to take me to the chamber again..." He wrapped his arms around his legs, pulling in his knees and curling into himself.

"Guess again." He smiled at him and Sean felt the temptation to try and read his emotions, but that wouldn't work in the drugged state he was in. It never did. He sighed, not answering this time. "Don't worry, I'll show you instead." The man stepped aside, and spoke a bit louder in the direction he came from. "All clear."

"Sean!" The dreaded voice rang in his ears like it always had. Lingering.

"Stop." As Tirin approached the bars, Sean shut his eyes tightly. "Don't come any closer."

Sean didn't see it happen, but with what he could hear, he swore Tirin had ripped the bars apart. They clattered and dropped onto the ground. "What the hell has he done to you?"

"Please. Stay away." Sean backed up against the wall. He knew what came next. Antic always came next.

"You're hurt." Tirin's voice was uncharacteristically soft. Sean knew it was a lie. It had to be. Tirin took a few steps closer.

"No. I don't want to see you. I know it's you. It's always you."

"Sean, please. I swear it's me. I came to get you out of here." Tirin knelt down in front of him. He reached out a hand and Sean flinched away.

"Don't. Just let me believe it's him for once." He looked at him, his eyes peering into his. If he had to go through this, he'd keep Tirin's image there for as long as he possibly could. Tirin sat down in front of him, respecting what he'd said. He'd never done that before. Sean held his gaze. "If you touch me, it won't be you anymore."

"Sean, they drugged you. I'm not going anywhere. I promise." Tirin's eyes softened. He stayed there patiently for a moment, just letting him have space.

"Why won't you just let me have peace?" When Tirin looked at him confused he continued. Even if he thought it was pointless, it got it off his chest. "I see you everywhere.

I even hear your voice when you're not here. I know it isn't you, and the second you come close, I know I'm right, but I can't seem to break away from the foolish wish I have that it's really you. I need it to be you. That's why you can't come any closer. For once I just want it to stay you."

"I need you to trust me." Tirin held out a strange look-ing type of needle. Sean's eyes darted between what looked like a torture device and him. "This will help with the drugs."

"Please, I don't want you to go away again." He tried to back up further but the wall kept him from doing anything but shuffling his feet against the ground.

Tirin reached out a hand and Sean pulled away for as long as he could before the back of his head hit the wall and Tirin's hand fell gently on his face. Sean squeezed his eyes shut. Apologies never made Antic any less merciless but he somehow couldn't help but try. "I'm sorry. I've told you that over and over again. I'm so sorry."

"You have nothing to be sorry for Sean. You've been there for me even when I didn't deserve it. Now I'm here for you."

Sean looked up. He'd never been happier in his life to hear his voice, to see his eyes. His real eyes. *Tirin*. He stumbled over himself, pushing off the wall and crashing into him in an attempt to hug him tightly and never let go.

Tirin's arms wrapped around him tightly. "What has he put you through?"

His eyes felt heavy. "You don't want to know."

Tirin held him tighter. "I swear I'll kill that bastard." Sean felt a spike of pain prick his back as Tirin shoved the needle of counter drugs into him. He looked up at him with teary eyes. "This should clear your mind soon."

Sean felt the haze of his mind clear slowly. It took all of five minutes to feel semi normal again. Still, part of him wanted to make sure it was really Tirin. He observed his aura, reading his emotions. The black smoke of his presence was a normal occurrence. Somehow there was something else in the dark haze, something more power-ful. "You did it…"

"We can talk about that later." The blond guy said, still standing outside the cell.

He should've been embarrassed that all of this had played out in front of a stranger, but Sean couldn't bring himself to care. He shifted against the chains, the sound of the rattling making his head ache a little. He looked at Tirin's object attached to his ear. The earring had changed. That's when he knew he'd gotten it right. Tirin had bound himself to the Necrotanian object.

The blond guy sighed dramatically. "Are you going to get him out of here already? We don't have all day." He turned to Sean. "I could've had you out faster but brooting over there insisted on coming with me."

"What did we say about keeping your big mouth shut Tempest?" The dark glow around Tirin's eyes spread a little down the veins in his face.

"Yeah, yeah. Whatever." Tempest put his hands up de-fensively. "On with it then."

Tirin lifted Sean's arms. In an instant, he was breaking the chains around his wrists with the heat in his palms from his new full object. He took a mental note at how much better he already was at using the object than Sean had ever been himself at using anything.

"Can you stand?" Tirin asked, helping him up.

"Probably not until the drugs clear up more." Sean's voice came out uneven.

"Fuck." Tirin cursed. He wrapped an arm around him, helping him through the bars. Sean focused on his touch for a moment. There was something in his aura. Something that made it hard to imagine pulling away. It was like there was some kind of energy pulling them together.

"What's your plan?"

"We either fight Antic side by side, or we merge the objects in the process."

Sean smiled weakly, amused that Tirin had a plan and stuck to it for once, even if it wasn't thought through all the way. "Good plan, but how exactly do you propose we do that? I'm drugged and neither of us know how to combine the objects."

Tempest pinched the bridge of his nose. "That's not the plan."

"That part doesn't matter right now. Let's just focus on getting you out of here."

Sean leaned against him, not resisting the help in the slightest. He smiled, a bit of warmth in his chest. "You came for me."

"I wasn't going to let you die." He felt Tirin tighten his hold around him as he spoke. "Don't you ever pull that shit again. We're stuck together, remember?"

"I'm here too, you know." Tempest said, starting down the hallway.

Tirin helped him down the hall to the large door that led to a long stairwell. For once, Sean let him help without questions or any hesitation at all. After all they'd been through, it felt natural to be that close to him. He'd convinced himself that Tirin would want peace, but he supposed he was never the type to let things go easily. His stubbornness outweighed anything else, even rational decisions. He was glad for that part of him. Glad that even in his worst moments, Tirin was the kind of person he'd come to trust and count on. The kind of person who would be there for him if he ever needed him.

***

Tirin practically had to drag him out of the dungeon. His body felt numb and sore all over. He dragged his feet occasionally, his mind still recovering from the fog of the drugs. By the time they'd reached a place for him to rest, his body almost gave out underneath him. Tirin steadied him, setting him slowly down on a table in one of the rooms of the lowest castle floor.

He might as well have collapsed against it. Tirin and Tempest exchanged some conversation, but Sean's mind was too tired to process it. After they had what looked like a small argument, Tirin placed a hand gently on his cheek. "Get some rest. We'll keep watch."

Sean didn't even have the energy to protest. As soon as he heard his words, his mind took it as permission to lose consciousness. He closed his eyes and instantly felt himself drift off into sleep.

Chapter 18
Tirin

"Can't you just do the thing already?"

Tirin scoffed as Tempest rolled his eyes dramatically. "Unless you know how to merge the two most powerful objects in Vermillia, then no, I can't just 'do the thing'."

Sean shifted a little under his touch. Tirin kept a constant hand over him, making sure he felt safe enough to rest. His attention drew then to the odd connection he'd been feeling since they reunited. There was some kind of energy now pulling them together. It was like the objects longed to be together again. Like just being near each other activated some kind of long forgotten need to be whole.

It wasn't the actual merging of the objects that scared him. It was the unknown of what would happen after.

The continent itself would change but that wasn't even the worst part. He couldn't stop wondering what would happen to the two of them. Surely there would be some kind of consequence, and it wouldn't be that simple. *And then what?* Would they then be the rulers of Vermillia? Would Seprati and Necrotan decide to unite? All of that seemed problematic. He couldn't imagine ever being on the throne even if he'd wanted to bind to the Necrotanian object his whole life.

His mind drifted back to the conversation he'd had with Sean on the backroads of Necrotan before he'd been taken. *Before he'd given himself up*. He looked down at Sean's peaceful sleeping expression, and all at once he felt the wish come back to him. The dream of running away from all of this. At least Sean's mind could be quiet for once while he slept. He couldn't help but feel like he deserved at least that much after everything. He'd argue with Tempest over and over again if it meant that he could secure Sean even just a few more minutes of sleep.

"Look, you might not have thought any of this through, but I have. Stop being a pain in my side and just listen to me. Even with the two objects, it's not smart to go after Antic guns blazing immediately. Especially when Sean needs to recover some of his strength. Even then what were you planning on doing if you did defeat him? Taking the throne or something?" Tirin grew quiet as Tempest spoke. He was right. None of what he'd been doing lately was helpful at all and rushing in was a terrible idea.

"Ok so what's your plan then?" He reluctantly decided to hear him out.

"We go back to the underground and regroup with the others. We let Sean recover while we come up with a solid plan to defeat Antic and more importantly a plan for what comes after that. You don't just high tale a revolution, you have to take it one win at a time."

"Fine." Tirin kept his eyes on Sean's sleeping form as he spoke. *As long as he's safe.* He slowly maneuvered his arms underneath Sean and picked him up off the table. Sean's arms seemed to instinctively wrap around his neck in response to the change in gravity as he leaned his head against his chest. He found himself questioning everything as they made their way to their planned escape route, holding Sean like he was some fragile thing he couldn't bear to lose.

***

Tirin spent the hours during Sean's full rest, right by his side. He wouldn't dare leave him, even if they were supposedly safe in the 'Underground'. A code name for a meeting spot the members of the revolution held most of their operations at. Tirin had a hard time believing it all before, that the revolution was real, and that it could've come about so quickly just becuase of Sean's mistake. Of course, being there, surrounded by people doing things left and right to prepare for what they thought would be a turning point in their push for change, made it feel absolutely real.

Tempest had explained to him over and over again how the revolution had been working behind the scenes a long time before Antic had been chosen for heir. They had never fully chosen the name, partly because the movement wasn't big enough. After Antic became heir and Sean stole the object, the movement grew in popularity. A lot of people saw Sean as a guy who made a bold statement. The one who pushed for change in a way no one else dared to. Of course Tirin knew the truth. Sean had made a mistake, and it costed him everything.

The way the members glanced his way every now and then, looking at Sean like he was their hero made his heart pick up just a little faster every time. Mostly because he knew Sean wasn't one to handle pressure well, and after whatever Antic had done to him, he would be in no position to lead anyone, even if they were expecting him to. He went over again and again in his head what he would say to explain it to him.

Hey dork, instead of waking you up a few minutes later, it's been hours and we took you to an underground place you don't recognize where people believe your mistake was a revolutionary push for change. Oh yeah and by the way these people now expect you to be some hero and lead them.

Of course not. As Sean began to stir on the small cot next to him, he had no idea what he was going to tell him. He convinced himself that the only thing that mattered was if he was safe. They could handle things later, as long as they were together.

He moved his hand that had been resting on Sean's chest to the side of his face, gently running the back of his fingers along his jawline. "Hey, sleepy head."

Sean hummed and pressed the side of his face against his hand. "Mmm..."

He felt his chest warm at the sound. "You're going to be the death of me, you know that?"

Sean spoke, keeping his eyes closed. "...Did we win yet?"

Tirin smiled affectionately. "I've already won." It was true. He'd gotten him back. He'd saved him. Sure he was acting like a sap, and part of him hated that fact, but another part of him didn't care. All that mattered was that gorgeous smile Sean gave him that he swore could've made his knees weak for a moment.

Sean peaked open his eyes, looking up at Tirin with a fond expression. For a moment he held his gaze before he looked around and seemed to realize they were somewhere different. "Where... are we?"

"It's called the Underground. It's a long story, but don't worry, you're safe here."

"What are all these people doing here?"

Tirin hesitated. "They're trying to fight for change. They're calling it a revolution."

"Is your friend a part of it?"

Tirin scoffed "Tempest? I'd hardly call him a friend, but yes. Actually he's one of the leaders of the movement."

Sean raised an eyebrow. "How'd you convince him to help save me?"

"I didn't have to. Let's just say he's taken a liking to you."

Sean looked even more confused than before. "Me?"

"Did he help you get the Necrotanian object?"

"Sort of. He's Veira's fiance."

Sean's eyes widened. "Viera is engaged to that guy?"

Tirin laughed. "Trust me I was just as surprised as you were."

Sean paused for a moment before speaking again. "What now?"

"Now we figure out how to merge the objects and kick Antic's ass."

Sean gestured to the people rushing around them. "I'm assuming they'll handle the ass kicking part?"

"It looks like it.

"What about us? I don't even know where to begin merging the objects."

Tirin held up his hand and channeled the smallest bit of his object power to the tips of Sean's fingers. "We'll figure it out. I can feel that the objects want to be together. It's like some kind of charged current between them." He'd felt it from the moment they were in the same room together. The object's sparking just beneath his skin, pulling him to a strange connection.

His thoughts were jumbled quickly by a voice coming from behind him. "He's awake!"

He cursed under his breath, preparing himself to comfort and defend Sean if needed.

Chapter 19

Sean

No one had ever looked up to him, much less admired him in his entire life. Now just about everyone around him looked at him like he was the coolest person in the room. Of course what else led to it other than his worst mistake. He didn't have the heart to tell them. Then again he felt he'd disappoint them anyway if he tried to go along with the notion that he was some revolutionary world leader. He couldn't help but think about the possibility that came with it though.

What if he could live up to it? What if he could convince himself he was some kind of hero? What if, for the first time, people believed in him for the right reasons? It was all a bit hard to think about. Especially when his head felt like it could explode in the aftermath of the drugs.

In the hours after he'd woken up, he'd been introduced to more people than he could count. Some leaders of the cause, some volunteers, some just regular people wanting to make a difference. *A difference in a revolution named after himself.* That part still felt strange.

Tirin hadn't left his side since he'd woken up. He stood by him like some kind of security guard, glaring at people who asked too many questions. Still, there was that charge of something whenever they'd get too close. A spark of some kind of electricity when they'd brush shoulders or hands. He'd choked it up to the objects wanting to be together, but how much of it was caused by his own feelings, he couldn't decide.

They had decided that priority one was merging the objects. Dealing with Antic could come later, provided they actually were able to achieve the merge. What would happen after that entirely depended on what would change once the Neutral object was created. That kind of powerful merge could theoretically be too much for the two of them. There was so much danger in that. Sean had made it his hourly thought process. As a certified overthinker, he found himself immersed and worried about every single possibility as a result of the objects' strong call to each other.

He'd always found it difficult to be alone in the past, but now, being alone felt entirely different. Being away from Tirin for any extension of time felt like an eternity. Every moment of separation created a stronger pull between them until they were close enough to relieve it a bit. Usually that meant some form of physical interaction. Sure it was an excuse to be close to him, but the absolute longing he'd feel when they were apart was something he couldn't get over. In a similar sense, he started noticing that he could sense where Tirin was at any given moment. He could feel when he was near, even if they weren't in the same room. At some point he felt like the energy between them clouded his mind a bit, making it hard to focus on anything else.

Sure his feelings for Tirin were complicated, but he wasn't *that* lovesick for him. After he had spent a day making a full recovery from the effects of the drugs and had gotten used to the odd energy between them, it became increasingly difficult for him to separate his own feelings from the pull of the objects. They ended up sleeping in the same bed in the underground, unable to ignore the pull enough to sleep separately. They were used to it anyway after having to share a tent for so long, but Sean didn't think he'd ever be used to going to bed with Tirin's arms around him.

"In that big head of yours again huh?" Tirin's voice shook him out of his thoughts.

He shifted in his arms, keeping himself comfortable. "Yeah..."

"Penny for your thoughts?" He gently ran a hand through Sean's hair, the motion soothing and filled with care.

"We need to figure out how to merge the objects soon. I just don't know how much longer I can handle the energy between us. That aching feeling if we aren't close enough."

"Are you saying you hate being close to me?" He teased.

"I didn't say that."

He chuckled. "So then what's wrong with it?"

Sean rolled his eyes, though he couldn't help but let a small smile grace his lips. "I'm being serious."

"OK Mr. Serious, we'll figure out how to merge the objects eventually, and until then you'll have to suck it up and deal with being close to me."

"You're impossible." Sean nudged his chest with his hand. "You can't honestly tell me you're enjoying this that much." The idea was foreign to him.

Tirin sighed. "Fine. You want me to be serious?" The hand in his hair traveled down to hold the side of his face. "Is it really that hard to believe that I want to be as close to you as possible?"

Sean instantly felt his face heat up. "What?"

Tirin held his gaze without hesitation. "You heard me."

He felt himself tense. "...why?"

Sean noticed the look that flashed in his eyes. The same look of vulnerability he'd given him back in the temple. "Honestly, when you were captured...seeing you in the cell like that, chained up and broken... I think it did something to me. I don't ever want to see you like that again, and something in me would do whatever it takes to keep you safe." He paused, tracing the rest of his face with his hand. "And maybe some twisted part of me thinks the best way to do that is to be as close to you as possible."

Maybe it was his own feelings, or maybe it was the objects pull between them, but Sean felt himself drifting closer to him, as if he couldn't control his own actions. He spoke a bit breathless, "...but, how close is too close?"

Tirin pulled his face gently closer with his hand. He made no effort to hide the way his eyes drifted down to his lips. "Are you looking to find out?"

After everything they'd been through, his own answer shouldn't have surprised him the way it did. He'd been thinking about the moment their lips met since it happened, and after he'd saved him from Antic's prison, the only thing he could feel was a need to be closer. He was sure he could drown out Antic's words with Tirin's touch even as they played out in his head. *Any time anyone ever*

gets close to you again, all you'll be able to see in them is me.
He squeezed his eyes shut.

Tirin lifted his chin. "What is it?"

"Antic he–" his mind stumbled over itself to explain, "He's made it so he's everywhere in my mind…"

Tirin's expression darkened and he cursed under his breath. "That bastard. I swear I'll kill him," When Sean hesitated, his gaze softened. "What do you need me to do to make you more comfortable?"

He closed his eyes tightly once more. "I just want to forget."

Tirin continued to rub soothing circles along his cheek as he spoke. "Then let me help you forget. Let me replace every broken memory with our own."

His heart fluttered in his chest as he met his gaze again, that odd feeling of warmth he'd felt before returning in his chest. He felt himself lean in and yet, he still wasn't expecting his own body to betray him like it did. He'd barely blinked and his lips were on his in an instant. In that moment, he didn't care what it meant or why it felt so liberating. Any memory became the furthest thing from his mind. All that he could focus on was Tirin's hands running down his sides and clinging to his waist to pull him closer.

His mind blanked and he practically melted as their bodies met. His thoughts started fading in and out as he struggled to create any sense of thought other than the way he felt against him. As if he couldn't feel any greater bliss, he heard the soft sound Tirin made that he'd never forget. It quickly burned itself into his memory, drawing out a sound from his own throat before his mind could protest. He was certain right then and there that he hadn't wanted anything more in his entire life than Tirin. His lips on his body, His hands gripping his hips, his sent filling his senses.

***

He'd been right about his assumption. He'd never get used to waking up in Tirin's arms. As hard as it was to get his mind off of it, neither of them had time for that sort of reminiscing. They had agreed that they might be able to figure out how to merge the objects if they fought each other. Some part of it felt like old times.

Sean felt the steady burning in his hands as he shot a small blast across the cave towards him. Tirin swiftly moved out of the way and summoned a few skeletons to try and grab Sean by the ankles out of the ground. Having fought alongside him, Sean had grown to expect that move from him. He lunged forward, summoning a bit of the burning to his hands to heighten the effect of a standard punch. To no surprise, Tirin dogged his head out of the way and pushed Sean back with a grunt of force. Sean stumbled backwards for a moment before catching himself and planting his feet into the ground.

"Come on, you can do better than that." Tirin taunted.

Sean clenched his fists hard. "You got the object you trained for your whole life. Of course you can use it better."

"You're holding back and you know it."

He was right. Sean was afraid of hurting him, really hurting him. He was playing it safe by using the power he knew he could do well. If he tried to do anything more he wasn't sure if he could control what came next.

Tirin responded to his silence. "I don't want to hurt you, but I will if that's what it takes to get you to try harder."

Sean knew it was an empty threat. If it really came down to it, Tirin wouldn't push it too far. That of course didn't stop him from planting a quick, hard punch to his gut. He grunted as the wind knocked out of him.

He grit his teeth. "Give me a break."

"We don't have time for that."

He lunged at him, threatening another blow. Sean dodged out of the way and tried to surprise him with a kick to the side. Tirin caught his leg and used it to swing him to the ground. He felt the ruff dirt hit his back and the stab of pain that came with it. He barely had time to try and get up before parts of the ground under him started to rumble and glow darkly.

"Get up." Tirin commanded. Skeletal hands burst from the ground, and Sean picked himself up by his legs, swiftly moving away from them.

At that point he narrowed his gaze. He was getting sick and tired of being knocked around like a rag doll. He knew he couldn't summon any type of creature, Tirin could easily counter that with his own so he focused on smaller parts of creatures instead. He thought if Tirin could summon only arms from the ground then surely he could summon a single part of a creature too. Though he'd never seen what he thought to do ever done before.

"Oh I'll get up alright." He channeled the burning sensation of the power towards his back, creating a small space between him and a portal. It opened and the back end of a winged creature sprouted out, claw like arms gripping his sides. Then he was in the air, commanding the creature to fly him up. Admittedly, he hadn't expected it to work at all. He assumed his expression reflected that because Tirin seemed impressed and equally suspicious of his words.

"Are you going to keep running or are you going to attack me already?"

Sean grit his teeth. "You asked for it." He channeled a large burst of energy through his hands, aiming it straight towards him. Tirin countered with his own burst of power. The dark and light energy collided with each other in a small flash of electricity. Sean's whole body lit up with an odd kind of spark he recognized. The pull of the objects seemed to strengthen at that moment. Then, he knew what to do.

He broke the blast, moving out of the way as the remainder of Tirin's burst hit the wall of the underground. He landed on the ground panting as the winged creature retreated back into the portal. His mind spun in all different directions as a small bead of sweat gathered on his face.

"I think that was it." He managed between breaths.

"You think we have to combine the objects energy like that?"

"It's worth a shot."

Tirin took a couple steps closer to him. "You do realize how dangerous that would be right? We'd have to channel all the energy we could right at each other."

Sean sighed, looking down at his hands for a moment. "I think we both knew we weren't going to get out of this unscathed..."

Tirin put a hand on his shoulder. It felt odd to him to be on the receiving end of it for once. "Break for lunch?"

Chapter 20

Tirin

Despite the fighting and responsibility, Tirin was finding it hard to focus on the present moment. His mind practically reminded him of the previous night's events every chance it got. Even through the course of the fight it was hard not to focus on anything else but the rush. They had figured out a possible way to merge the objects, but it almost didn't feel like a step forward. He hadn't expected it to be easy, but he also hadn't planned on risking his life for it.

After eating lunch with Sean, a thought occurred to him. *Why not just keep the objects as they were?* Of course that would mean he'd have to be the ruler of Necrotan and he was by no means a good leader. He knew that. He also knew that absolutely no one else would humor that idea. Sean could be a good leader, even if he couldn't see it within himself, but Tirin on the throne would be a disaster and that was no secret. Perhaps they could balance each other out, Tirin the war lord and Sean the noble policy maker. He chuckled to himself knowing that would never happen with the ball of anxiety Sean was, and part of him found that endearing.

Even if they wouldn't be the worst rulers Vermillia had ever seen, the members of the underground and Sean's Rebellion would never agree. They were pushing for real change, not just helping the two idiots who started it all.

"What's so funny?" Sean asked as they walked through the dimly lit halls of the underground.

Tirin shook his head, an unintentional smirk on his lips. "Nothing. I just can't imagine ever having to actually be the ruler of Necrotan."

Sean chuckled. "That would be a disaster."

"Exactly."

"But you know after this, someone has to step up and lead." He said it as if he'd been contemplating the fate of Vermillia all day.

Tirin shook his head. "But you and I won't have to worry about that."

Sean raised an eyebrow. "You don't think we'll make it out of this?"

"Of course I do, I just meant—" Tirin cut himself off trying to gather his words. He sighed, reluctantly admitting the truth he'd been wanting to say. "Didn't you say you wanted to run away?"

Sean stopped walking and Tirin turned to face him. "And leave the country to handle itself?"

Tirin put his hands on his shoulders. "I'm sure the members of the rebellion could handle it. They probably already have a plan by now. Let yourself have peace for once, just like you said back in the alley. Just you and me, somewhere no one could bother us." He knew he was being a bit desperate but he didn't care. Sean deserved that life he asked for, and much more than that. Seeing the way Sean's face went pink, he knew he'd said the right thing.

"You're serious?" The way Sean said it more like a hopeful plea made is heart twist.

"I'm serious, I promise."

A small smile grew on Sean's lips. "If we make it out of this, I'll hold you to that."

Tirin ruffled his hair. "*When* we make it out of this, I'll make sure I don't disappoint you."

***

They'd met with Tempest and a few other leaders of Sean's Rebellion to explain their working theory about merging the objects. After that it was settled. They'd have to find a large clear space and concentrate all the power they could into a single blast of energy towards each other. Tirin hoped that would be enough. Whatever came after depended on how the objects reacted to being together again within the same universe.

After all of the meetings and more exhausting fighting with Sean, the last thing Tirin wanted to see was *her*. Jordan stood outside the door of the room Tirin and Sean had been occupying for the last couple of days in the underground. She was leaning against the wall fidgeting with her nails. He sighed.

"What do you want?"

She smiled, not looking up from her nails. "I just want to chat with an old friend. I'm a part of the revolution you know."

"Is that supposed to make me mad or something?"

She laughed. "Not everything is about you Tirin. I'm here for the same reason everyone else is. Things need to change. It just so happens that the revolution involves you."

Tirin rolled his eyes. "If you're not here because of me, then what are you doing outside my door?"

"I've been informed of the new plan to merge the objects. I just came to wish an old friend good luck."

Tirin took a step closer and crossed his arms. "I don't need *your* luck."

She pushed herself off the wall and approached him. She lowered her voice, her tone less guarded. "Oh come on, stop being so bitter. There's a lot I could do to piss you off but I haven't done any of that. I cared about you when we were together a year ago. That kind of care doesn't just go away whether you want it to or not. I'm just saying I don't want you to get hurt ok?"

Tirin sighed, letting his anger melt away. He knew he was being unreasonable. Jordan wasn't at fault for the way he'd treated her a year ago. He was lost when he was with her. Lost in a kind of way that made his actions question-able. He knew that. "I'm not going to get hurt."

Her expression grew hesitant, like she hadn't expected such a calm response. "I know you're afraid. You don't have to act like you're not."

He held his breath, hoping he wouldn't regret what he was about to say. "I'm sorry Jordan."

"What?" She raised an eyebrow.

Then he let words fall out like melted butter. "I'm sorry for how I've treated you. You were right back at the gas station. I've been an asshole to you. I was afraid of getting close to anyone and I'm sorry you got hurt in the crossfire of my internal battles."

She paused, searching his gaze. "Who are you and what have you done with Tirin?"

Tirin rolled his eyes again. "Don't make me repeat myself. I've been reflecting a little, ok?"

She chuckled. "Sean really has influenced you."

He hesitated. *Had Sean changed him?* He didn't know if he wanted to face that idea. Just like Jordan said, he knew he was afraid. Afraid of letting anyone so close. Afraid that he'd lose who he was in the process. Yet at the same time, he was afraid to lose him. He thought the warring in his mind would've silenced by now, but it only seemed to become more complicated.

It made sense really. He'd been told all his life that connections were bad. That they clouded your mind and made you act differently. That they could be used against you. While all of that was true, his time with Sean had taught him that not all of it was a bad thing. Maybe change could be good. Maybe it was worth the risk of losing him.

"I'm sorry too. I should've been more patient with you. Maybe I'm a little salty that I wasn't the one to help you, but do me a favor and don't push him away like you did me, ok?"

"I won't." He was determined to keep that promise.

"You better tell him too before you go out and merge the objects."

Tirin shifted on his feet. "Tell him what?"

"That you love him."

He froze up, unable to process the idea that he could *love* Sean. Getting close to him was one thing, but *loving* him was something else entirely.

She punched his shoulder. "You're so dense sometimes. Just don't go and get hurt, ok?" Then she put out a friend-ly hand. Tirin took it with a firm shake. Jordan turned and started to walk down that hall. "If you make it through this mess, you'd better let me know you're alive."

"I will."

Chapter 21
Sean

He read Gem's emotional state out of habit. The crease between her brows had made him nervous, but reading the calming waves of the blue energy surrounding her eased his mind a little. The way she sat at the two person table in the dining area gave away her intentions. He'd known ever since she'd invited him to have a coffee with her that she wanted to talk. Not just any kind of talk, the kind of sibling talk that was serious.

He took a seat in the chair in front of her. "Alright, what is it?"

She chuckled and took a sip of her drink. "Can I not have a coffee with my brother?" She slid the one she'd gotten for him across the table.

Sean picked it up and took a sip, letting the hot chocolate liquid he'd ask for sooth his nerves. "Don't give me that. I know when something's up."

She put a hand up in mock surrender. "Alright, you caught me. I've been thinking lately."

"About?" He asked, egging her on.

"About my position in the VAA." When Sean visibly tensed she spoke again, keeping her tone light. "Relax, I'm not going to try to hand you over again, I promise."

Sean let out a breath he was holding. "Good."

"I think I'm going to quit."

Sean's eyes widened. "But you've finally gotten a good position." Sure he didn't like the way the VAA ran things, but he wouldn't care as long as it made his sister happy.

"You know, I've always felt like I had to prove myself here. Like I had to strive for some kind of power or some kind of recognition, especially after the family object was given to you." Sean lowered his eyes. "But with people from the normal continent, I can just be myself. No one there has any kind of power or object. Everyone is just trying to live out whatever dream makes them happy, not whatever makes them powerful."

He met her gaze, finally understanding where she was going. "You're moving?"

"I'll at least be staying there for a while. I'd like to figure out what I want with my life. What I *really* want."

Sean smiled. He'd love nothing more than seeing her happy in a life she wanted. "Maybe you'll meet the love of your life and open a flower shop."

She laughed. "I was thinking more along the lines of a physical training business. I've always been into personal health."

It was true. She'd even taught Sean how to get in shape for the trials. The more he thought about it, the more he could see it. "Just don't forget where you came from."

"Trust me, I don't think I could ever forget how my brother roped me into fucking up an entire continent's politics."

And just like that they spent the rest of the time laughing and trading memories from when they were kids. By the end of it all She gave him the tightest hug he'd ever experienced. "Don't you dare do anything I wouldn't do."

He returned the embrace just as tightly. "I won't."

"I'll see you before I go after you merge the objects. Do me a favor and take care of our resident angry couch potato while I'm gone."

He laughed thinking the nickname didn't suit Tirin at all. "He'd punch you if he heard you call him that."

"I know."

***

"I said, I love you."

"I love you too, dork. I'm your brother, I'll always have your back, remember? Brothers in heart." Sean laughed.

"Dam you and your thick skull." He stepped closer, something in his eyes Sean didn't recognize.

Sean rolled his eyes playfully. "Ok, cut it out. I can't read your mind. Just tell me what I'm missing."

He reached for his hand, a kind of simple connection the two of them were familiar with. In the past it wasn't as comfortable but after a long period of what he called 'conditioning' Sean had grown more used to his touch and noticing when he needed it. Sean took his hand slowly, rubbing the back of it gently. He was concerned for him. He hadn't ever seen him try to be this serious in the face of his own laughter. That look in his eyes, it only made his concern grow.

"Forget it."

"What's wrong? I know that look. You're never this on edge."

He hesitated before his eyes darted to the ground. Sean was used to his body language by then, and he knew exactly how to comfort him. He'd grown accustomed to the exact ways he liked to be distracted, and which things would tick him off or make things worse, which he would avoid. He sat down on the grass, the cold night air brushing through his hair. He patted the spot next to him, smiling. The two of them were quiet for a long moment. He sat down next to him and looked up at the sky, taking a deep breath just like they had practiced. Hard topics always left him feeling a bit paralyzed and that led to him being unable to speak through it. Sean always knew how to comfort him just enough so he could get whatever was bothering him off his chest.

"Take your time." Sean gave him a soft smile, still holding his hand in a firm and grounding way.

He took a few deep breaths. "I...I'm not sure how to explain."

Sean gave his hand a gentle squeeze. "Then don't. I'll be here for you either way."

He sighed. "You know how the world always seems against us?"

"I think that's just the way we can sometimes perceive it." As soon as he said it, something in his mind screamed at him that it was the wrong thing to say. He felt a nervous shot straight to his gut.

"You're wrong. That's how people want us to see things. They want us to be blind to their manipulative actions." He squeezed his hand back, not as gently.

Even as the warning alarms blared in Sean's mind, he hadn't learned what he should and shouldn't say around him at that point, so he spoke from the heart. "There's always more than one angle to look at things from."

He tensed, making the feeling in Sean's stomach tighter. "So you want me to make excuses for the way people treat me? For the way things are in the world? Why would I let them win like that."

Still, Sean's ignorance made him continue to try and be himself. "It's not for them, it's for you. Look at it differently for *your* mental peace, for *your* healing. I'm not telling you to excuse anything, I'm telling you to let it go for your own sanity."

"There you go again, talking like you know what it's like to be cast aside by people. Your family loved you, they took you places, your sister protects you when you need her. I don't have all of those things. You don't understand."

He let go of his hand and turned away from him. That churning in Sean's gut made him want to throw up at the thought of provoking him. He couldn't let him push him away, knowing what he might do to himself. "I thought you were here to help me, but maybe I was wrong. I have no one else, and if you won't help me then I'd rather not be here at all."

"Don't say that." There Sean went again, playing into it like a lost puppy coming back to an owner that didn't deserve him.

"Why not? It's true. Do I need to remind you that I have the scars to prove it?" He pulled up the sleeve of his hoodie slowly. Sean put a desperate hand on his arm, stopping the motion.

"Please, I didn't mean it like that."

"This is why it took me so long to trust you with them in the first place.I knew it would be a burden on you. I knew you'd want to leave me the moment I told you."

"You're not a burden to me. I swear it."

"Promise?" At the time, Sean wasn't able to tell the difference between real tears and fake ones. Tears came slowly down his face, his eyes blinking rapidly and squeezing tight a few times.

"I promise." Sean spoke with a desperate ache in his heart.

He took a deep breath, wiping the tears from his eyes. He turned back to face him. "You know, sometimes you're the only thing keeping me going..."

"I know..." Like every other time, Sean forced his arms open, a silent offer for a hug. Antic took the opportunity, almost knocking him over as he wrapped his arms around him tightly. Sean felt the water from his eyes through his shirt as he leaned his head against his shoulder, wondering how much more he could do to help him, to save him from himself. It wasn't until after it had all gone south that Sean had realized all of it was a lie. Some sick game Antic had played to pull him down from the happy place he was, straight to the depths of the earth with him. And the worst part, he'd fallen for it. Played the game blindly until it left him with nothing but broken pieces of his own heart that Antic had clawed out and walked away with.

Chapter 22
Tirin

Tirin felt Sean wake with a start, causing his arms to tighten around him instinctively. He forced himself out of sleep sitting up in bed with him, pulling him against his chest. That's when he felt the water pouring from his eyes.

HIs heart twisted as he heard Sean's panting breath. He brushed a thumb along his cheek to wipe away some of his tears. "Hey, easy. It's alright. You're safe." Sean clung tightly to him, burying his face into his chest. Tirin brushed a hand through his hair, his soothing motions laced with as much care he could give them.

Sean opened his mouth to say something through his breathing but all that came out was a broken sound.

"Shhh, It's alright. Just breathe. Listen to my heartb eat."He pressed his head against his chest before pulling the blanket further over him, trying to wrap him in it's warmth and comfort. He felt Sean take deeper and deeper breaths, his body relaxing against him. "That's it," Tirin wiped the last tear from his eye, "Bad dream?"

"A memory."

He brushed his thumb along his cheek. "Want to talk about it?"

Sean pressed his face into his hand. "I don't think Antic was always violent, but I think he was always a not so good person..."

Tirin pressed a kiss to his forehead. "That makes sense. You don't just become as violent as he is overnight."

"But there was a time when I was sure he was a good person. I thought I knew him. I thought he cared about me."

"Maybe he did, in his own sort of twisted way. What makes you say he wasn't who you thought he was?"

Sean turned his face and pressed a kiss into Tirin's palm, making his chest warm. "I don't think I was ever fully myself around him. I think I was just who he made me think I was. Looking back there's so many things I never noticed. So many times I changed parts of myself to make him happy."

He tightened his hold around him protectively. "You won't ever have to do that around me."

"And that's how I know he wasn't a good person."

Tirin raised an eyebrow. "What do you mean?"

"Because you've shown me what a good person really looks like."

Tirin held back a scoff. "You think I'm a good person?"

Sean smiled, something that made Tirin believe he was saying the right things. "You might be an ass sometimes, but I know you've got a heart in there, and you'd never want to *really* hurt me. Not like he would."

"I guess that's true."

"You're also how I know I never saw him as anything more than a brother."

"Is that so?"

"Because I know how it feels to care about someone in a different way now. In *this* way." He pressed a kiss to the crook of his neck.

His heart swelled with that same sense of warmth. He hated how it seemed so easy for Sean to make his mind spin. Somehow at the same time, he didn't mind it at all.

***

They'd chosen a large open field on the outskirts of Necrotan to perform the merge in. Since Tirin had become the official air and obtained the object through normal means of trial challenge, it was the safest place so they wouldn't have to risk going back through Seperati. Tempest stood by them, directing a few medically trained volunteers to be at the ready in case anything went wrong. Truthfully they had no idea what would happen and they needed to be ready for the worst.

It wasn't like there weren't several stories and legends about the Neutral object, but none of them ever talked about it being separated. How and why it actually happened was a complete mystery. No one even knew how long it had been that way, or who had done it. It was like some kind of past the world wanted to forget. After all they had been through, Tirin hoped the objects were not separated for a reason because if they were, they'd have to find out why the hard way.

He stood in front of Sean, watching as the same stream of thoughts likely plagued his mind. They met eyes. Tempest didn't seem to mind that they were taking so long to get on with it. Perhaps he understood the gravity of it all. Sean stepped closer. If that was the last time they might see each other, if something went wrong and they ended up trapped in something they couldn't undo, they needed to touch, just one last time.

Sean reached out hesitantly. Tirin pulled him into an embrace. "It's not like we haven't gotten ourselves into messes before." He tried to comfort him with light teasing, but in the end he knew how serious the situation was and he wasn't sure either of them could escape it.

"If I could go back and undo it all, I'd never get close to the object." Sean's voice broke.

Tirin felt an ache in his chest. "I wouldn't. I'd trade anything to learn what you've taught me. To be close to you."

Sean's arms tightened around him. "If you asked me ages ago, I would've never thought I'd be going out with you by my side. I wouldn't have it any other way."

Tirin leaned his head into Sean's hair, inhaling him for what could've been the last time. "We'd better do this before we never pull away from each other." He gave Sean one last gentle squeeze before reluctantly pulling away.

They separated, the burning pull of the objects towards each other, stronger than it had ever been. Once they were a decent distance away from each other, they took their stances, firm. Tirin nodded and gave Tempest the signal to count off. He kept his gaze on Sean the whole time as he heard the count down. *3...2...*

At first the explosion didn't register. As his view ob-structed between the clouds of smoke, he felt the heat of it all. Then he saw Sean on the ground and his world tilted. When Antic came into view beside him, and the corners of his eyes laced with red.

Chapter 23

Sean

His chest heaved without his control. He looked over through the clouds of smoke to see Tempest and the medical staff held up, fighting several Sepratain soldiers. Then he saw Antic and his world shook underneath itself. Seeing him, the crooked smile on his face, the unreadable anger, it reopened every wound he'd been trying to heal for the past week in the underground.

"Didn't I tell you I wouldn't let you escape me? I'm in your mind Sean. In the darkest corners."

As Sean tried to pick himself up, he realized just how much pain he was in. He was surprised he could hear Antic at all with the ringing in his ears. He forced himself to speak, his voice rough. "This is between us, there's no need for anyone else to get hurt Antic."

"None of that ever really mattered to me before, why would it now? You just think this is all about you and I don't you? Tell me Sean..." He lowered the blaster he'd been carrying. "...Why do you think I put the border laws in place? Why do you think I went through all that trouble to keep the separation?"

Sean hesitated, pushing himself up onto his knees. "Because if the objects merge you'll be powerless."

Antic laughed, a sharp and deep sound. "Sometimes certain types of people just don't belong together. *You* taught me that. Whether the objects were merged before or not doesn't matter. They were separated for a reason, and I'm not going to find out why just because some people don't like how I do things." He raised his weapon, pointing the blaster end right at Sean's face.

"If you kill me, the people I care about won't stop until you're dead."

"Something I'll have to deal with later, but at least I'll have the Sepratain object on my side. Maybe even your family pendant."

"That's close enough asshole." Tirin's voice rang out from behind Antic, his eyes glowing with the power of his object.

"You hurt me, I shoot him. I'd be careful if I were you, it's not like your medics will be able to save him while they're *caught up*."

Tirin tensed. "You shoot him and I kill you. You won't get what you want, even if your soldiers manage to kill me afterwards."

Sean let the power of his object flow freely through him, his eyes and palms sparked with a kind of burning sensation. "You can't do it anyways. You might be a violent piece of shit, but you can't bring yourself to kill me. You want me to suffer alive."

Antic tensed and narrowed his eyes. "You don't know me Sean, no matter how much you think you do."

"Do it then. Shoot me." He dared. He knew it was a stretch, but there wasn't anything else he could do. He would either die right there and then, or he wouldn't.

Tirin's eyes went wide and Sean could feel his panic through the object connection when Antic shot a blast straight at his face. For a moment time stood still. He began to see things, memories. Gem when they were kids, Antic's sense of humor, *the good times*. He forced his eyes shut. He couldn't let it happen. He wouldn't let his life flash before his eyes. Not when he was this close to getting the life he knew he deserved. He felt a burst of adrenaline course through him.

When he opened his eyes he had Antic by the arm. The blaster had missed him and created a burn mark in the grass where he had been kneeling. It took him a couple seconds to realize Antic's body was stiff. He looked down to see a baseball sized hole practically burned straight through his chest. He felt the tingling in his hands, the remnants of the power he'd used. It was only after Antic collapsed that he realized he was the one who did it. He caught him in his arms, holding him against his shoulder for support.

Antic laughed, his voice horse as blood spilled out of him. "You were... never really one for goodbyes... but you always wanted to live... more than I ever did..."

He felt his body grow lifeless against him. He must've cried out because the next thing he felt was his vocal chords straining in his throat and his eyes blurring with tears. That's the thing about people like Antic. No matter how badly they've treated you, it still hurts to lose them.

***

The remaining Sepratain soldiers backed off after Antic's death. Since he challenged him first, technically defeating him meant Sean was the new air. That didn't stop Tempest and Tirin from hurted a few more of them, probably too caught up in the heat and emotion of the moment to realize they'd stopped attacking.

Sean stared down at Antic's lifeless body, frozen in place, tears streaming down his face. He'd lost more than just his old friend. He'd lost the life he desperately hoped they could've had. The life some part of him still thought pos-sible if he could've changed him. He didn't know when Tirin had ended up engulfing him in a tight embrace, but he buried his face into his shoulder.

"You did the right thing."

"But it hurts." Sean croaked out.

"I know."

By the aching in his chest, he knew Antic's last words would be something that would replay in his mind forever.

Chapter 24

Tirin

It took the whole rest of the day to get things back into motion. Tirin spent the entire time glued to Sean, comforting him the best he could while Tempest and some other members of the underground looked for a new location. The explosion had created a decent sized crater in the field they'd started in. Honestly it was an excuse to give Sean the time he needed to pull himself together. None of that stopped the aching pain in his chest from tormenting him at the way Sean caved into himself like a scared animal for the rest of the day. Tirin was there for him all the same.

The next morning when they both felt functional enough to perform the merge, they traveled a further distance from the underground on the outside of Vermillia's center line. It seemed more fitting to do it there at least.

Word had quickly spread on Antic's death and a small crowd gathered to watch the merge. Tirin couldn't blame them even if it seemed dangerous. They were about to make history, and he'd want to see it too if he wasn't the one doing it. If the rest of his supporters knew what Antic had done, they probably would've been there too, and yet something told him they wouldn't be so quick to change their minds.

They stood a decent distance away from each other. They didn't linger much this time, not wanting something else to get in the way. As Tirin gave Tempest the signal to count down he thought about what Jordan had said. *Did he love Sean?* He'd hated the thought of losing him, so much that he could've gone headfirst into Antic's soldiers if he wasn't so focused on making sure Sean was safe the day before. If they weren't dead by the end of the merge he wanted nothing more than to live out his days with him, unbothered by the rest of the world.

If loving someone meant never wanting to leave them, then maybe he did *love* Sean. He'd always thought he was incapable of the feeling, but Sean taught him otherwise, along with all the other things he'd taught him. How to feel again. How to be vulnerable. How to manage his anger, and now, how to *love*. If it all ended badly, he found himself glad that his last thought would be that. He focused on that thought as Tempest finished the countdown. *He loved him. 3...2...1...*

He felt the cold prick of the Necrotanian object spark through his veins. He focused every ounce of it he could muster through his palms. The power of the blast nearly knocked him backwards, but he managed to steady himself in a firm stance. Across from him, Sean did the same. The energy met in the center, causing a force to push against the very air itself around them. He could feel his earring, the physical form the object manifested itself in, fading away.

The blast might have only lasted a few minutes but it felt like ages with the amount of energy it took to keep that kind of power from bursting out of him like a bomb. It took almost everything in him to keep it as a concentrated beam especially with the sensation that continued to pull him towards Sean like a black hole. The power swirled in the center where the blasts met, pulling everything he had into it. Still he could feel that it wasn't enough.

With a loud grunt he pushed everything he had into it one last time. Then everything was gone. He'd spent so long feeling the constant cold prick of his object abilities that he almost felt empty as his earring crumbled away into ashes. The center of the blast materialized with a bright light into a large portal extending at least a couple hundred feet above the ground. That's when he realized he was still alive. He looked across the field, seeing the relieved expression on Sean's face. Nothing else mattered as they rushed at each other. Maybe not for Vermillia, but for them, it was over.

Chapter 25
Sean

Sean stared out the window at the small garden they'd been growing for the past few months. They rarely received any mail, wanting to keep their location decently unknown, but Sean enjoyed the letters he and his sister often sent each other. He wrote back to her, sitting at the small table in front of the window.

Dear Gem,

I'm glad to hear you've got the funds to start up your business. I knew you could do it. You and your girlfriend should come visit us in the summer and we'll celebrate. As for what's up with us, our garden is coming along nicely. We've managed to befriend a stray cat who often lurked around our property fence. We've named him Tibs. He's great company and he keeps the snakes away like a brave little soldier. I'll admit I never thought I was a cat person, but he's got the soul of a wolf in him. If he could bark, he probably would.

The garden does well in providing for us the essentials, but Tirin and I have gotten jobs in the small town near us to fill in the gaps. For a small town they really do like to talk. As much as I hate hearing about it, I can't seem to escape the news about the Neutral object's portal and the things that keep coming out of it. I'm just glad you're safe in the normal continent. We've thought several times about moving over there too, but in the end we settled to stay here. I still have the family pendant, and now that things are finally settling down for us, we aren't ready to pick up and move. I know you understand.

As for the comment in your previous letter, No, we're not getting married. It hasn't been that long and while I don't ever see myself leaving Tirin, who has the money for a wedding? Besides, we are try-

ing to keep ourselves hidden. No way we're going to get into that kind of legal binding and potentially expose ourselves. Maybe the name change would at least be nice. You're still the only one who gets to know where we are. Perhaps this summer we can have a cute little ceremony ourselves but for now, I'm content the way things are.

Anyways, tell me how your company works out. I'd love to hear more of what you've been up to outside of that too. What's your new apartment been like? Is your girlfriend really that afraid of spiders? Details please and thank you.

You're favorite and only brother,

Sean

He heard the front door to the small house shut. "Hey, how was work?" Tirin groaned dramatically after letting Tibs inside and hanging up his keys. He walked over and wrapped his arms around Sean from behind. "That bad?"

"The other employees just don't know how to get their shit together." He leaned his head against Sean's shoulder.

Sean chuckled. "At least you don't have to be the king of Necrotan."

"Can't argue with that." He pressed a kiss to his cheek.

"Would it make you feel better if I made your favorite for dinner?"

He smiled, an expression Sean still wasn't used to seeing on his face. "I'd like that. Need help?"

"If you want."

He headed into the kitchen. "I'll start chopping."

Sean smiled to himself. Tibs rubbed against his legs. He ran a hand along his back a few times, scratching behind his ears. He watched as Tirin wrapped an apron around his waist. He'd never get used to that either. He'd always imagined he would be the one cooking when they started the garden, but Tirin was twice the chef he ever was. Sean stood and drew out a bottle of liquor from the fridge, pouring the two of them a small glass and mixing it with some lime juice he'd set aside. He handed Tirin his and raised the glass above his head.

"To our peace." Tibs meowed in the middle of his sentence, wanting more attention. Sean laughed. "And our new little addition to our home."

Tirin smiled at him, a smile he knew he'd never tire of seeing. "Alright dork, I'll play along with your cheesy toast." He raised his glass. *"To our peace."*

About the author

Alen Gracen is a transgender queer author of LGBTQ+ fantasy romance books. He is also a college student and has two loving emotional support cats that sit at his desk as he writes his stories. Much of what he writes comes from his own experiences, making a lot of what his characters go through quite relatable to him. In sharing his work with the world he hopes he'll inspire others to keep going through the hard times and create what makes them happy above all else.

More of Alen Gracen:

Instagram: @alengracenauthor

Email: alengracenauthor@gmail.com